Inky Odds

SELECTED FICTION WORKS BY
L. RON HUBBARD

FANTASY
The Case of the Friendly Corpse

Death's Deputy

Fear

The Ghoul

The Indigestible Triton

Slaves of Sleep & The Masters of Sleep

Typewriter in the Sky

The Ultimate Adventure

SCIENCE FICTION
Battlefield Earth

The Conquest of Space

The End Is Not Yet

Final Blackout

The Kilkenny Cats

The Kingslayer

The Mission Earth Dekalogy*

Ole Doc Methuselah

To the Stars

ADVENTURE
The Hell Job series

WESTERN
Buckskin Brigades

Empty Saddles

Guns of Mark Jardine

Hot Lead Payoff

A full list of L. Ron Hubbard's
novellas and short stories is provided at the back.

*Dekalogy—a group of ten volumes

L. RON HUBBARD

Inky Odds

Published by
Galaxy Press, LLC
7051 Hollywood Boulevard, Suite 200
Hollywood, CA 90028

Printed in the United States of America.

ISBN-10 1-59212-286-8
ISBN-13 978-1-59212-286-8

Library of Congress Control Number: 2007903618

Contents

Stories from Pulp Fiction's Golden Age

A ND it *was* a golden age.

The 1930s and 1940s were a vibrant, seminal time for a gigantic audience of eager readers, probably the largest per capita audience of readers in American history. The magazine racks were chock-full of publications with ragged trims, garish cover art, cheap brown pulp paper, low cover prices—and the most excitement you could hold in your hands.

"Pulp" magazines, named for their rough-cut, pulpwood paper, were a vehicle for more amazing tales than Scheherazade could have told in a million and one nights. Set apart from higher-class "slick" magazines, printed on fancy glossy paper with quality artwork and superior production values, the pulps were for the "rest of us," adventure story after adventure story for people who liked to *read*. Pulp fiction authors were no-holds-barred entertainers—real storytellers. They were more interested in a thrilling plot twist, a horrific villain or a white-knuckle adventure than they were in lavish prose or convoluted metaphors.

The sheer volume of tales released during this wondrous golden age remains unmatched in any other period of literary history—hundreds of thousands of published stories in over nine hundred different magazines. Some titles lasted only an issue or two; many magazines succumbed to paper shortages during World War II, while others endured for decades yet. Pulp fiction remains as a treasure trove of stories you can read, stories you can love, stories you can remember. The stories were driven by plot and character, with grand heroes, terrible villains, beautiful damsels (often in distress), diabolical plots, amazing places, breathless romances. The readers wanted to be taken beyond the mundane, to live adventures far removed from their ordinary lives—and the pulps rarely failed to deliver.

In that regard, pulp fiction stands in the tradition of all memorable literature. For as history has shown, good stories are much more than fancy prose. William Shakespeare, Charles Dickens, Jules Verne, Alexandre Dumas—many of the greatest literary figures wrote their fiction for the readers, not simply literary colleagues and academic admirers. And writers for pulp magazines were no exception. These publications reached an audience that dwarfed the circulations of today's short story magazines. Issues of the pulps were scooped up and read by over thirty million avid readers each month.

Because pulp fiction writers were often paid no more than a cent a word, they had to become prolific or starve. They also had to write aggressively. As Richard Kyle, publisher and editor of *Argosy*, the first and most long-lived of the pulps, so pointedly explained: "The pulp magazine writers, the best of them, worked for markets that did not write for critics or attempt to satisfy timid advertisers. Not having to answer to anyone other than their readers, they wrote about human beings on the edges of the unknown, in those new lands the future would explore. They wrote for what we would become, not for what we had already been."

Some of the more lasting names that graced the pulps include H. P. Lovecraft, Edgar Rice Burroughs, Robert E. Howard, Max Brand, Louis L'Amour, Elmore Leonard, Dashiell Hammett, Raymond Chandler, Erle Stanley Gardner, John D. MacDonald, Ray Bradbury, Isaac Asimov, Robert Heinlein—and, of course, L. Ron Hubbard.

In a word, he was among the most prolific and popular writers of the era. He was also the most enduring—hence this series—and certainly among the most legendary. It all began only months after he first tried his hand at fiction, with L. Ron Hubbard tales appearing in *Thrilling Adventures, Argosy, Five-Novels Monthly, Detective Fiction Weekly, Top-Notch, Texas Ranger, War Birds, Western Stories,* even *Romantic Range.* He could write on any subject, in any genre, from jungle explorers to deep-sea divers, from G-men and gangsters, cowboys and flying aces to mountain climbers, hard-boiled detectives and spies. But he really began to shine when he turned his talent to science fiction and fantasy of which he authored nearly fifty novels or novelettes to forever change the shape of those genres.

Following in the tradition of such famed authors as Herman Melville, Mark Twain, Jack London and Ernest Hemingway, Ron Hubbard actually lived adventures that his own characters would have admired—as an ethnologist among primitive tribes, as prospector and engineer in hostile climes, as a captain of vessels on four oceans. He even wrote a series of articles for *Argosy*, called "Hell Job," in which he lived and told of the most dangerous professions a man could put his hand to.

Finally, and just for good measure, he was also an accomplished photographer, artist, filmmaker, musician and educator. But he was first and foremost a *writer*, and that's the L. Ron Hubbard we come to know through the pages of this volume.

This library of Stories from the Golden Age presents the best of L. Ron Hubbard's fiction from the heyday of storytelling, the Golden Age of the pulp magazines. In these eighty volumes, readers are treated to a full banquet of 153 stories, a kaleidoscope of tales representing every imaginable genre: science fiction, fantasy, western, mystery, thriller, horror, even romance—action of all kinds and in all places.

Because the pulps themselves were printed on such inexpensive paper with high acid content, issues were not meant to endure. As the years go by, the original issues of every pulp from *Argosy* through *Zeppelin Stories* continue crumbling into brittle, brown dust. This library preserves the L. Ron Hubbard tales from that era, presented with a distinctive look that brings back the nostalgic flavor of those times.

L. Ron Hubbard's Stories from the Golden Age has something for every taste, every reader. These tales will return you to a time when fiction was good clean entertainment and the most fun a kid could have on a rainy afternoon or the best thing an adult could enjoy after a long day at work.

Pick up a volume, and remember what reading is supposed to be all about. Remember curling up with a *great story*.

—Kevin J. Anderson

KEVIN J. ANDERSON *is the author of more than ninety critically acclaimed works of speculative fiction, including The Saga of Seven Suns, the continuation of the Dune Chronicles with Brian Herbert, and his* New York Times *bestselling novelization of L. Ron Hubbard's* Ai! Pedrito!

Inky Odds

Inky Odds

T HE calm and dignity of the Shanghai Office of World Press had all the aspects of a church—providing the church was being hurled aloft by a typhoon. Men sat at their desks, girls at their typewriters, and business went on as usual—as usual, because, practically unnoticed, George Graves was tearing the place into fragments with a lusty bellow. And the reason—also as usual—was Bat Conroy.

"Where's Conroy? Where's Conroy, I say! Damn it, are you all deaf? *Where's Bat Conroy?*"

For an instant Graves recalled that he had visitors and turned with a hypocritical smile of apology. One was a lady of perhaps twenty-five years, dark and glamorous, and with an air of sorrow which made her twice as lovely. The other was a baffled little woman, Gwen Fairington's maiden Aunt Agatha.

"I'm sorry. I can't ever seem to find anybody," said Graves. And then to the whole office again, yelling from the door of his own, "Where the hell is Bat Conroy? Are you all dead?"

A scared secretary who was of a size and appearance which made it probable that George Graves would some day eat him without salt, lifted a tremulous voice. "He's covering the Japanese attack on the Twelfth Route Army north of Changkow, sir."

"Where?" roared Graves, as though he had received a personal affront.

"North of Changkow, sir."

"Oh, lord! Lord in heaven deliver me! Oh, by all the saints and devils and demons and— That's gratitude! That's gratitude for all I've had to put up with from Bat Conroy! Here's the biggest story of this confounded, out-of-date war, and Bat Conroy is north of Changkow! Here's a story with a heart-throb, pathos, drama and big copy, and Bat Conroy is covering some peanut-sized battle north of Changkow!"

"You . . . you sent him yourself, sir," quavered the secretary.

"*I* sent him!"

"Yes, sir. It's the b-b-b-biggest b-b-battle we've had in months, sir. You said so, sir, when you sent him."

"Stop stuttering! Of course I sent him! That's right—lay all the blame on me! Now listen! This is Gwen Fairington and her Aunt Agatha. Does that mean anything to you?"

"Y-Yes, sir. She's the heiress to the toothpaste fortune, and her husband deserted her and came to China and got l-l-l-ost—"

"Right! That's news. That's news, do you hear? We've found her husband for her and she's come to us for help. And where is he? Where *is* he?"

"I don't know, sir."

"He's up in Fu-Chiang, that's where! Up beyond four battle lines. And he's a doctor, so what's he doing? He's trying to keep the Americans at Fu-Chiang from all dying of cholera. He's in deadly danger and there's no way to rescue him. But we're sending a boat upriver. Upriver through shot

4

and troops and bombs and rapids and whatnot, to rescue Bill Fairington and restore him to his wife who has searched for him for two years. Have you got that?"

"Y-Y-Yes, sir."

"All right. *All* right. Then grab an office telegraph and send word to Bat Conroy that I don't care how many battles he's covering, to return here immediately and take charge of this. Tell him it's the greatest story of the war. Tell him it's terrific. Tell him it's dangerous. But get him back here as fast as he can travel." The secretary was about to scuttle away when Graves stopped him. "Has he filed about that battle?"

"No, sir."

"Huh! Hell of a lot of good *he* is lately. Battle going on and he hasn't got the story in! Now beat it!"

Mopping his brow, George Graves sank down at his desk. "I don't know how I ever live through this," he told Gwen Fairington. "Nothing ever goes right. Nobody is ever where you want him. And International Service is scooping us on everything that breaks. Some day I am going to blow out my brains. I feel it in my bones."

A sigh of sympathy came from Gwen Fairington. "But you are being lovely to us. I shall never forget it."

"It's . . . it's all a little confusing," said Aunt Agatha. "This Bat Conroy—"

"You've heard of him, dear," said Gwen. "He's the best World Press has."

Aunt Agatha made a fluttery motion with her hands. "But this will be very dangerous for him. He might be killed!"

"No more than us, dear," said Gwen. "We are going on that boat with him. I've searched too long for Bill to—"

"*Chief!*" came an agonized wail from the outer office, and a reporter loped in with a telegraph blank. "Chief, I've just found out that International Service filed that Changkow yarn five hours ago and the battle has hardly started! It's that Perry Lane!"

"Oh! Oh, oh, oh!" cried Graves. "That Bat Conroy has been scooped again! Hell and snowing cats! If he gets killed going upriver on this trip it will damn well serve him right!"

Along a shell-ripped road, below a sky as leaden as the spumes of powder gas which soared above concealed but raging batteries, Bat Conroy wended his happy way.

China was in flames! Millions were dead! Starvation, disease, flood, fire, agony and disaster avalanched across the land!

China was in flames and Bat Conroy warmed his capable hands before the conflagration and grinned a happy newshound's grin. He shot out sizzling copy and heard the snick of bullets by his ear with an ecstasy another man might experience at the opera. Bat Conroy was not bloodthirsty. In itself, disaster did not make him happy. His detached, human self might even writhe in sympathy for these doomed forfeits to a major political error.

But blood made news, and there were those who said that the great Conroy of World Press had not been born at all, but had been cast in a linotype and had come smoking and half-molten into the world to talk in headlines, to eat newsprint, and to bleed, not blood, but ink.

He was well over six feet, though the way he had of standing—a careless, cheerful way—reduced his height. He had an eager, overjoyed air about him which, some said, not even the news of his own death could have changed. His nose was a prominent part of his not unhandsome face, and when he was excited his nostrils quivered like those of a high-strung horse—and he only got excited when he smelled a headline in the making. His eyes never seemed to take in the immediate vicinity, but were forever looking just beyond the horizon where, they seemed to hope, a much bigger battle might be killing a much larger number of men. He had neither combed nor cut his yellow hair in the memory of his associates, or perhaps that was an illusion caused by his habit of exhibiting his emotions by smoothing, tearing or tousling that yellow mop.

Just now his long military trench coat was splattered to a dun color by the mud of the alleged road. His abused felt hat was hauled down over one eye to keep out the spatter of rain which had come to bog down guns and horses and so prevent the Japanese from following up the retreating Chinese and putting a final period to a couple of divisions of troops.

This war had been going on for years. It would probably continue to go on for years. It was no longer front page, and yet it still had to be reported. And Bat Conroy, knowing that, lived in perpetual hope that it would take a sudden dramatic turn and again loom three inches high on page one. At times

7

he even went so far as to wonder just how he could go about making it that exciting, but, so far, he had no usable ideas.

His joy was being melted by this rain, little by little. For when the Japanese had driven the Chinese out of this town, it had seemed possible that the Chinese would be followed up across hard, coverless country and annihilated to a man. That would have made a story. But this rain!

Here was a tank, its treads half swallowed by muck. There was a gun limber with a squad of the lads in mustard straining at its bogged wheels. Nearby was a tangle of men and equipment, an infantry brigade, gazing dolefully at caked boots and thinking with despair upon the probability of complete starvation. Further along was an ammunition supply column, overrunning its own front line and trying to get turned around where there was no room to turn, before Chinese artillery found it and scattered the landscape with Japanese.

There were two houses in this town which were not burning, and one of these had no rear. Of the others, there were a few walls, a few gravel piles bedecked with various bits of personal property, including bits of human beings.

Up high, a shell roared and exploded in a fountain of earth and men somewhere to the right. The next shell came down so near that it did not howl at all. There was a swift whisper and then a shattering roar, and the last half of the ammunition train exploded all together to ornament the sky with pieces of trucks and cases and unlucky drivers. Down past Bat Conroy a wounded horse came screaming, scattering the bogged brigade through its center. A shot cracked and the horse went down. A little officer raced up and down like a wild thing and in a high, panicky voice told his company to be calm. There came a certain note in the air above, Bat Conroy dropped on his face in mud, and then came a blast so furious that it seemed to invert the very earth. The company was gone. So was the little officer.

Bat Conroy dug himself to the surface and spat out the yellow mud. Well! The Chinese were making a good retreat of it, anyway. "Twelfth Route Army Retreating in Good Order—"

Zingarowwwwwww! Mud and bricks and the triple explosion faded into hot, dry smoke, leaving baked earth where a stalled camion had been.

Japanese artillery bellowed and blasted, and the far-off moan of an airplane motor brought them on their target. Bat Conroy lay for a while in an acrid-smelling crater, on the theory that a gun pointer usually changed his sights between salvos. Near and far, for the next twenty minutes, shells continued to land, but at longer intervals. The Japanese artillery, too, began to decrease in volume. And then the gray skies opened in earnest and the chilly flood reached with cold fingers down Bat Conroy's neck, no matter how tightly he buttoned his collar. He looked at his watch and found that it was three in the afternoon, a fact which surprised him, for he had supposed it around ten in the morning. Simultaneously his stomach confirmed the passage of time and, without really taking his mind off his story, Conroy got out of the crater and began to scout for food.

Bat Conroy drew a long breath, for it was quite apparent that the Chinese had made good their retreat and that the Japanese would now only mop up and dispose of a few snipers and possible spies. He would find something to eat and then he would burn up the highway—or what was left of it—if he could find a car—for Changkow and file his story.

For a moment a small barb of worry nagged him; a little anxiously he looked around him, half-expecting to discover his nemesis of the last four months.

Every time he had something hot to file of late, he felt this way, the way an inventor feels when his task is done and he begins to realize that another man might get the invention to the patent office first. Conroy was getting wholly superstitious about Perry Lane.

He had no inkling of Perry Lane's appearance, knowing only that he was a competent war correspondent on the staff of International Service who had appeared suddenly and without fanfare upon the Chinese front to especially bedevil the days of Bat Conroy. Five times in six weeks Bat Conroy had filed a hot story, only to have Graves, at Shanghai, scathingly inform him that International Service had released the yarn some hours before, and invariably under the byline of Perry Lane.

Bat Conroy had tried to figure out all manner of explanations, even that of telepathy, so that he was almost afraid to think a story before he filed it.

But General Shimizu, that morning, had informed him that he was the only correspondent with the Japanese in this vicinity and that the one called Perry Lane could not, therefore, be around. Conroy solaced himself with this information now, and walked through the mud and rain and debris, nearly convinced that he had, for once, an exclusive. Of course, he would have liked some additional angles. There was a lot of stuff being printed about what the Japanese were doing to their prisoners, and possibly, if he could get the story, World Press might be mollified, despite his recent tardiness.

With this in mind, Conroy eased off the road toward a group of disconsolate Chinese under Japanese guard, intending to interview some of them and then wait and find out what happened.

An officer with a red band on his cap looked with hostility at Conroy. "I am sorry—very sorry—but you cannot linger here."

They were standing beside a high, if battered wall, the exterior of some school yard that offered some small protection from the rain. This officer's refusal was all that Bat Conroy needed to make him stay.

"I am Conroy, of World Press."

The officer looked closely at him. "Papers?"

Conroy showed his line passes and the officer became very courteous.

"I am sorry. I was given orders not to let anyone see these prisoners. But if you are Mr. Conroy—"

"Thank you," said Conroy and turned to address a Chinese officer who, stripped of sidearms and coat, dismally awaited his reunion with his ancestors. But before Conroy could speak, there came a crashing rattle beyond the wall. Two machine guns were going in there. They stopped. Conroy looked sharply at the Japanese officer and then turned to enter the arch.

"No. No. So sorry! You cannot go in there!"

"Thank you," said Conroy, and walked in.

The yard was about a hundred yards long, surrounded by

the wall. Two or three hundred prisoners were herded into one end of it, and perhaps fifty corpses were caved in at Conroy's right. Two machine gunners sat dispassionately upon their tripods and waited for the next batch to be sorted out and stood up.

The officers had men hauled out of the mob at random, clearly with the intention of executing all of them at length, but giving those who still lived something to think about to occupy their time.

Into the present batch was pulled a White Russian officer. His shoulder was damp with redness and he wore no cap. But he was grandly condescending to his captors. Two Chinese snipers were next.

Then the guard hauled out a white girl from the mob and thrust her into the newly forming group!

She was speaking in very rapid Japanese—so fast that Conroy could scarcely follow her. But she did not seem to be frightened, merely concerned.

"But I tell you this is a mistake! I am not a Russian. I am an American. I . . . I am an American missionary, and if you will cable President Roosevelt I'm sure he will tell you—"

"Quiet!" barked a Japanese officer.

"But the President and I are old friends! And besides, how could I be a White Russian! Born in Lansing, Michigan, USA!"

A guard thrust her toward the wall.

She disconsolately took out a pack of cigarettes and, offering one to the White Russian officer, lit his and her own.

"But the President and I are old friends!
And besides, how could I be a White Russian!
Born in Lansing, Michigan, USA!"

"This is highly irregular, Ivan. Your name, of course, *is* Ivan, isn't it? They ought to have a court-martial and then a blindfold, and somebody ought to wave a sword before they fire and say it is all for the good of the Mikado."

"It is a very messy day on which to die, madame," said the White Russian. "One will make such a soggy corpse. But then, since birth, I have known that I would some day come to a bad end, and so now I have no longer to worry about it. First my vast estates, and now my life. Ah, but then that is fate."

"Officer!" said the girl. "Officer, don't you want my last words?"

"Quiet!"

Conroy, throughout all this, had been stunned. She had spoken Russian to a Russian, Japanese to a Japanese, and she must be terribly sure of getting out of this, for certainly no woman had *that* much nerve. And what a strange girl she was to find up here in the drenched plains of Central China! She belonged on a stage on Broadway with that face and figure. She was as blond as he was, and quite as splattered with mud—

She looked toward the gate and saw Conroy, and then she stood up straight and quickly masked the joy which had nearly burst through to the surface. Instead, she registered tearful relief.

"Oh! My brother!" she cried in Japanese. "My dear, long-lost brother! How I have searched for you!" And, her arms outstretched, she came past the guard and straight toward Conroy. The guard took a moment to see whom she was addressing and so failed to block her. And the next instant

14

Conroy had her arms around his neck and was being kissed tearfully.

"What is this?" cried the officer in charge.

"My brother," sobbed the girl. "I have found him at last!"

"Who are you?" demanded the officer of Conroy. "Don't you know that this woman is a White Russian spy?"

"He is Conroy, of World Press," said the officer at the gate to his comrade at arms.

"Conroy?"

"Yes," said the other Japanese. "I have inspected his papers."

"Ah! I am *so* sorry. But is this woman really your sister?"

"Er . . . uh . . . ouch! Certainly. Yes, indeed. My long-lost sister. (Bite me again, my dizzy jane, and I'll drown you!) Of course she is!"

"Ah! I am so sorry . . . so very, very sorry!" said the officer. "If there is anything we can do—"

But if this strange feminine waif of the battlefields was quick on the uptake, Bat Conroy was quicker. He had intended stealing a staff car or something and getting to the river, and then taking a launch down to Changkow. But there would apparently be no more battle in this vicinity, so—

"I do not know," said Conroy, "how I can overlook this outrage. I was on the verge of reporting this as a sweeping Japanese victory. But if you celebrate a victory by trying to kill my innocent sister—well!" And he started to draw the girl through the arch, trying not to notice the startled and admiring way in which she now regarded him.

"No, no!" said the officer. "Wait! There is my colonel. I am sure we can explain. She was—"

"I am sorry," said Conroy. "This matter cannot be so lightly forgiven."

They reached the colonel, and the officer tried to explain and save his own face. But while he was doing it, a staff car came down the road, the enemy having left the place, and General Shimizu was signaled to a halt.

"There is nothing to be said," said Conroy. "This is a shocking incident, and I deeply regret—"

"What is this, Mr. Conroy?" said the general.

They told him, all talking at once, and when he finally understood he seemed very anxious.

"Mr. Conroy, if there is anything we can do to make you forget this—"

"Nothing," said Conroy grimly.

"Not even . . . not even a plane to wherever you want to go?"

"Well—"

Shimizu turned to his staff captain and had him scribble a note. And then, with apologies and assurances, the general drove away.

Bat Conroy and the girl slogged down the road toward the last outpost of Japanese Imperial Air Force planes. The rain was letting up now, but the mud was deeper than ever, churned by tanks and boots and guns.

Conroy looked wonderingly at the girl. She wore a beret at a jaunty angle, no matter how wet it was, and she had a Chinese officer's cape about her shoulders, which helped some in keeping out the rain. Her face, thought Conroy, showed signs of sweetness, but it could be bold enough. It was, he told himself, a rather exciting kind of face.

"Who are you?"

"Me?"

"You."

"Oh—just me."

"I mean, what's your name?"

"Name?"

"Certainly, your name!"

"Do you like Alice?"

"Yes. What's that—"

"My name is Alice. Alice Greyson. Isn't that a good enough name?"

"Well—yes. Who *are* you?"

"Me?"

"Look, do we *have* to do that?"

"No. I'm a ballet dancer, marooned."

"Yeah! Sure! A ballet dancer! Marooned in Central China!"

She looked at him with a puzzled frown. "You don't believe me?"

"Oh, sure! Of course I believe you. Hell's bells! If I had a nickel for every ballet dancer I've run into while following the Japanese fortunes of war, I would be able to buy scads of yachts!"

"You think I'm lying!"

"Well?"

"But it's the truth. It's the gospel truth! I swear it! I was with a show, and when the war broke out we were stranded. I have just now succeeded in getting through the Chinese and Japanese lines in an attempt to return to the coast. Now do you believe me?"

17

"Dog bites man!" Conroy jeered.

"Sure! Dog bites man! The truth is stranger than fiction, and you know very well that this is a good news story. If my press agent were here he'd have it plastered all over the front pages. You believe me now, don't you?"

"Well . . . guess I'll have to. Have a cigarette?"

"I've got some, thanks."

"Since when can one buy American cigarettes back of the lines?"

"Oh, these? Why, I had six cartons when I was stranded, and this is the last pack." She skipped a pace in order to get in step with him. "You aren't very trustful, are you?"

"Oh, sure. Newspapermen are always such trustful guys!"

"Oh, so you're a real reporter!"

"Sure. I'm Bat Conroy, of World Press."

"That's a big news service, isn't it?"

"Biggest there is."

"And I'll bet you're the best reporter in it."

"Somebody has been talking, huh?"

She laughed and, from time to time as they walked along, she glanced sideways at him in a pleased, admiring way which did not seem to have any effect upon him whatever.

When they came to the edge of the flying field and Conroy had presented his credentials, she suddenly demurred.

"Oh, look! I'm not going with you!"

"But this will take us straight back to Shanghai. I thought you wanted to get to the coast!"

"Oh, no. I mean . . . yes, of course. But I've left a friend and . . . and some baggage and . . . and I really don't dare desert either of them. Now don't worry about me. You just run along."

"Okay," said Bat.

"Maybe . . . maybe we'll meet again some place. Maybe New York, huh?"

"Never can tell," said Conroy.

"Oh, yes. Thanks awfully for saving my life."

"That's okay."

"Wait. Thanks for the offer of a lift."

"That's okay, too."

She evidently couldn't think of anything else and so had to let him walk away toward the waiting bomber which had been placed at his disposal.

"Goodbye!" she called after him.

"S'long," said Bat Conroy.

Muddy and bearded and tired beyond thinking, Bat Conroy slogged down the Bund toward the glittering Imperial Hotel. He was rebellious. He was so tired that when fifty rickshaw boys had tried to give him a lift he had cursed all babbling rickshaw boys and walked.

Waiting for him was a bed spread with silk in a room all beautiful and clean and dry and quiet, with a bathroom that had a shower where hot water could be had just by turning the knob. And where his boy Wong did the knob-turning.

Behind him were five days of mud and bad food and no whiskey worth sniffing. No matter how high his enthusiasm had mounted to the sound of machine guns and exploding shells, he was now of the opinion—caused by reaction—that

19

anybody who ever wrote up a war ought to have his head removed and preserved in a museum as the top-piece of all lunatics.

Dog-weary, he didn't care about anything but half a dozen drinks, dinner and a bath, and then a sleep fifty hours long. And so it was that he almost ran straight into an immaculate party coming down the steps of the Imperial Hotel. He stopped, stupidly wondering what was blocking his way.

They stopped. Gwen Fairington's escort, a Marine captain, looked truculent. Aunt Agatha appeared disturbed. In glittering diamonds and creamy silk, Gwen Fairington drew back a trifle, as though afraid that this muddy, rain-sodden wreck of a man might soil her. The Marine captain interposed.

"On your way, panhandler. You'll get nothing from us!"

"Huh?" said Bat, reeling a little with the tiredness in his bones.

"I said beat it!" snarled the Marine captain. "You Bund grifters with your phony stories give me a pain. Squads right, and get the hell out of the way!"

"Oh," said Aunt Agatha. "Oh, the poor man looks positively starved. Give him something, Gwen!"

The Marine captain made a grunting sound of disapproval. Bat stared at the three of them, still wondering what it was all about and why they didn't get out of his way.

Gwen impatiently put her hand into her bag and drew out a silver Mex, which she handed to the Marine to give to Bat. And Bat, finding something being shoved into his hand, took it without knowing what it was. He watched the three go past him and on to the rickshaws at the curb. He looked long at Gwen Fairington, for he was coming around a trifle, stimulated by her beauty. One didn't see anybody like that in Shanghai these days—a beautiful, glamorous woman with a mysterious air of sorrow about her.

What was this in his hand? A silver Mex dollar? What the—?

"Oh," said Bat to himself, beginning to grin. "Oh! So I'm a panhandler!" He staggered up the steps and was about to hand the silver to the doorman when another thought entered his aching head. Luck piece. He'd keep it.

"Oh, I am so velly solly, Mlistah Conloy. No know." And the doorman grandly opened the door for him.

Bat looked back and saw that the party had pulled away. Gee! Wonder what her name is!

Too bemused by weariness first, and then thrown into reverie by the vision of that girl, Bat was up to the fifteenth floor and standing inside his own room before he next came to himself.

Usually Wong was very much pleased to see his bloss mastah home again from the wars, safe. But Wong was perspiring now, and his gleaming yellow oval face showed great agitation. He stood now in the middle of the floor, motionless.

Bat at first did not notice, but then, finding that Wong said nothing, stopped on his way to the bedroom and looked around. Seated comfortably in an easy chair and regarding Bat with a slight smile was a Japanese in civilian clothes. Behind him, squatted with his back in a corner and thoughtfully

21

sucking the muzzle of his rifle, was a thirty-day conscript soldier—sloppy and crude, but hopeful for violence.

"Mr. Conroy?" said the civilian.

"The same."

"I am J-42." The little Japanese looked very mysterious about it.

Bat sighed a deep sigh. Shanghai, ever since the little lads in mustard had come tromping in, had reeked with the espionage activities of the Japanese and had been jammed with Japanese agents. Had they been regular army it might have been different, but they were nothing more than civilians, even peasants, with more power than they had ever before possessed in their lives. And at such inopportune moments as this they popped up, went through papers, took one to police stations, confiscated baggage, and took great pains to insult one and all, especially white men.

"I am tired," said Bat. "I am tired and I need a drink and a night's sleep. Come back next August and I will tell you truthfully that it was really I that shot that Japanese soldier at the corner of the Bund and Nanking Road. Goodbye."

"Shoot soldier?" said J-42. "I do not hear about this, but it is very serious."

"I had to," said Bat. "He looked like a mule."

"Ah," said J-42, "you are being funny!"

"And you are being unnecessary. Wong, run me a bath and get me a drink and show these fellows to the door."

Wong trembled, but he held open the door. Neither J-42 nor the soldier bodyguard showed any inclination to move.

"Tomorrow," said J-42, "you go upriver."

"That's news to me," said Bat. "Maybe you've got me mixed up with Chiang Kai-shek."

"You go upriver. American Consulate Fu-Chiang in very bad condition, people get cholera, no got food. You go upriver."

"And if I do, what of it?"

"You had not better go, Mr. Conroy."

"Why not, if I'm supposed to?"

"Because I say you better not go. You go, something terrible happen to you. You, Conroy. You very great press man. Regrettable to have terrible thing happen to great Conroy. So sorry. Not better go Fu-Chiang. Excuse me."

"Don't be so damned mysterious! What's this all about? In the first place, I don't know anything about having to go, and in the second place, if I am supposed to go, I'll go. If I started to go, your whole army couldn't stop me. Now get out and stay out. I'm tired!"

"Hah! Maybe not army stop you. Maybe not. Excuse me, but you no better go. You go, you die. So sorry. Excuse me. Good night."

Bat didn't even look at them as they left. He wrapped his hand around a Scotch and soda and banished the matter from his aching mind.

The phone jangled. The phone rang and rang. The phone rang so hard that it almost fell off the table.

Bat Conroy sighed and reached forlornly toward it, then forgot about it and, snuggling down, went back to sleep.

The phone jangled.

The phone rang and rang.

"Oh, hell! I mean . . . hello," said Bat.

"Conroy! Where the hell are you?" shouted Graves.

"You must know. You called me."

"Where have you been?"

"Covering a battle."

Graves snarled, "You sound like you've been drunk."

"So what? I cover a battle for five days and then I take three drinks and go to sleep. Maybe I take six drinks. Maybe I finish off a whole bottle before I go to sleep. That's what covering a battle does to you."

"Where the hell is the story?"

"I filed it at Changkow."

"Sure. Sure you did, and I got it. But what's the idea letting International beat us by five hours, by ten hours, by a day, by a month—"

"Whoa! I filed as soon as the shooting was over. They *couldn't* have beaten us. I filed right there at Changkow!"

"Well, International got the story to the States and Europe and India and South Africa and the Sulu Islands while you were out getting drunk! That's what! While you were out padding your expense account and getting plastered. By heaven, Bat, I don't mind you're getting drunk, but I do mind your making the service pay for the drinks and then not filing a story on time—"

"All this on an empty stomach!" sighed Bat.

"I ought to fire you! Then you'd know what it was to have an empty stomach, you worthless, thieving stew-bum!"

"The top of the morning to *you*," said Bat.

"Did you ever hear of Gwen Fairington?"

"The toothpaste queen with the toothpaste smile?"

"Yes."

"Yeah."

"Well, listen. She's here in the office right now with her Aunt Agatha, see? And you're going upriver to Fu-Chiang on a boat she's chartering. She's found her husband that ran away from her."

"Oh, poor fellow!"

"Shut up and get dressed, and be here in ten minutes or you're fired!"

"Could I depend on that?"

"On what?"

"Getting fired."

"Shut up and get going!"

"You wouldn't even be decent enough to fire me?" said Bat. But Graves had hung up and the crack was wasted, a fact which threatened to spoil Bat Conroy's temper.

A cigarette was gently placed in his mouth and Wong lighted it and, being a very wise little Chinese, drifted away from there. But Bat Conroy, after a moment, decided he had had something nice happen to him. It was a hazy feeling, as illusive as the substance of a dream. Something nice had happened to him. What was it? A hot story? Story . . . story? No, he'd been informed that that confounded Perry Lane had gotten the beat on him with that battle, so it wasn't a story. Well, must be a woman then. Yes. Now let me see—

Oh, hell, yes. That girl on the steps of the Imperial last night, shoving a Mex dollar into his hand as if he were a beggar. Say, now, she *was* somebody nice to think about. Dark and tall and mysterious, and somehow hauntingly familiar of feature. Sure. But who was she? Would she be in Shanghai long?

That assignment! Now he'd have to leave Shanghai. Shucks, he'd call Graves and tell him to give the job to somebody else. Maybe that lady lived right here in this hotel—

"*Wong!*"

"Mastah?"

"Wong, you pot-bellied heathen, turn on the shower! Lay out my very best clothes! Give me my dressing gown! Order breakfast! Where's my mail?"

"No can do," said Wong sorrowfully.

"Huh? What's that?"

"No can do. Missee got dressing gown, use shlower."

"Missee got dressing—*Missee?* Say, what the cockeyed catfish are you talking about? Missee? In my suite? In my shower? Using my dressing gown?"

He was about to launch further questions when he heard a low, musical voice singing. It had been going on for some time, but he had been too foggy to think that it was any closer than the next suite. Somebody singing in *his* shower? Well! That *was* nerve!

> "Oh, the birdies have no feet in Mariveles,
> Oh, the birdies have no feet in Mariveleeees.
> The birdies have no feet,
> They were burned off by the heat,
> Oh, the birdies have no feet in Mariveleees!"

Huh! There was something terribly familiar about that voice.

"Why didn't you throw her out?"

"No can do."

"Did . . . did she come in with me last night?"

"No, bloss mastah. She come maybe fi-six o'clock. Say she go sleepy-sleep on couch. She very wet, very muddy. She say she Number One pal bloss mastah. You say no wake this morning. Time fi-six o'clock. Wong glive one piece blanket, she sleepy-sleep—"

> "Oh, the carabao has no hair in Mindanao,
> Oh, the carabao has no hair in Mindanao,
> Oh, the carabao has no hair,
> 'Cause he is too doggone bare,
> Oh, the carabao has no hair in Mindanao."

"Kick her out!" said Bat. "Kick her out. I don't care who she is or how she got here. Kick her out!

> "The men they wear no—"

"Hey!" cried Bat. "Hey! You!"

> "The men they—"

"Hey!"

"Am I being paged?"

"Come out here!"

"Right now?"

"Right now!" Then hastily, "Don't you dare!"

"My master's voice!" And a white arm reached around the edge of the bathroom door and filched his dressing gown

27

from the chair. A moment later, almost swallowed in the folds of the silken garment and fluffing out her blond hair, she came mincing into his presence.

"Top of the morning to you, sir."

Bat's jaw was sagging. How . . . how in the name of fifteen little white mice had she gotten all the way from the plains above Changkow down here to Shanghai?

"What are *you* doing here?"

"Well," said the girl, helping herself to a cigarette and seating herself on the edge of his bed, "thereby hangs a tale."

"What did you come to my room for?"

"My dear man, you evidently do not understand the true impulse of the cosmopolitan. He does what the Romans do. The Chinese have a quaint custom and I am, after all, in China. When one saves the life of a Chinese he is then, forevermore, the property of the person who saved him. And so—"

"That's nonsense!"

"Nonsense in another land, but in China, my dear newshound, it is true. All too true!"

He was very angry with her but—well, now that she had some of the mud washed off and was rested, there was a very great deal to say for the way she looked. Her face *was* bold, but still it had sweetness in it. And, certainly, it was the most intelligent face he had ever seen on a woman. There was something about her manner which struck a sympathetic chord in his own heart. But . . . yes! He was angry with her.

"You'll ruin my reputation!" he snarled.

"May I be pardoned, sir, if I titter?"

"Well, it doesn't look nice."

"But you do. Even when you are cross. But you neglect your duty as a host. Wong—" and she volleyed Chinese at the servant which sent him scurrying for the nearest telephone to the dining room.

She picked up the pack of cigarettes and, with a smile over her shoulder at Bat, wandered from the room with the statement, "You know, you'd look much better if you shaved off five days' worth of beard." The sitting room door closed behind her.

Dazed, Bat Conroy bathed and shaved. And while he dressed he pondered the situation. How could she have gotten from north of Changkow to Shanghai in time to arrive here at five or six o'clock in the morning, when he himself had not arrived from Changkow itself until nearly ten the night before?

He couldn't understand that.

But when he was seated across the breakfast table from her, she had no further information to offer on the subject.

"You know," she said, "I have always longed to have breakfast with a handsome man. To breakfast with the great Bat Conroy."

"Well, if you put it that way—"

"And besides, I do not like to leave Shanghai hungry."

He was a little annoyed at his own sudden alarm. "You're leaving Shanghai?"

"On a boat."

"Oh, say—! When?"

"I'm not quite sure, but I think it is today."

29

"But wait a minute! What about money and . . . and clothes and—"

"I have my ticket, and a diamond I always pawn."

"Oh. A diamond!"

"I bought it myself," she smiled.

"You did? Well!" Why the devil, he asked himself, did he have to feel so relieved about that?

They ate in pleasant silence for some time—she occasionally stealing a look at him and he wondering what made him feel so keenly about the news that she was leaving Shanghai today. He ought to be mad at her. He *was* mad at her, taking such liberties with his room and reputation! But still—that news *did* have a depressing effect.

"I . . . I'm sorry," he said, "but I think I've forgotten what you said your name was."

"Are you sure?"

"Yes. I remember. But what's that got to do with it?"

She seemed to be pondering and then, brightly, "It's Dorothy. That's it. Dorothy."

"Doesn't seem right. I seem to recall—"

"Maybe I told you my first name. Nearly everyone calls me Dorothy."

"Where will I see you again?"

"Oh, I really don't know. Not exactly, that is."

"And you are sure you've got enough money and tickets and—"

The phone jangled. The phone rang and rang. The phone almost knocked itself out.

"Hello!" said Bat in a pained voice.

"Aren't you on your way yet?" roared Graves. "Have you got to keep us waiting all day? It's almost time for lunch."

"Then eat lunch," said Bat practically.

"Bat Conroy, if you're not over here in five minutes, you are very distinctly fired!" Bang went the receiver at the other end.

"He means it," said Bat. *"Wong!"*

Wong came streaking in with cane and hat and gloves.

"If you need anything," said Bat, "go down to Wing On Department Store and tell them to charge it to my account."

"Are they used to that?" she said.

"Don't be ridiculous!"

"Wait! Aren't you even—well, after all you saved my life."

He gave her a perfunctory kiss, started away from her and then suddenly turned back and gave her a real kiss. The last glimpse he had of her as he raced out the door, she was sitting just as he had released her, looking straight ahead with starry eyes, her lips slightly parted.

She was, he told himself, a very clever and a very beautiful woman.

But he really should be mad at her.

It was with a shock that he found Gwen Fairington and the woman who had given him the Mex dollar were one and the same. He bowed when she and Aunt Agatha were introduced to him, and was rather surprised that they did not recognize him. But then, he had very little in common, just now, with a bearded, muddy bum in a torn trench coat.

"Very pleased, I am sure."

"The pleasure is all ours," said Gwen Fairington graciously.

Bat sat down and Graves began to talk about the project in an excited, propagandizing tone of voice. But Bat just sat there and looked at Gwen Fairington.

This was funny! For months he had not even glanced at a woman, and now, suddenly, two of them were hurled at his head. This Gwen, of course, was a perfect lady. She had background and breeding and culture, and an air which made men want to go find some joss sticks and burn them at her altar. Imagine Gwen Fairington turning up at five o'clock in a man's room. Ha!

"What the hell are you laughing at?" said Graves, annoyed at the interruption of his long discourse.

"Who?" said Bat.

"You! I tell you that this is the most serious thing you have undertaken and you say 'Ha!' what do you mean, 'Ha'?"

"Never said a word," said Bat.

"Huh! Well, now, have you got it all straight?"

"What?" said Bat.

"My God, I've been talking to the man for half an hour and he says 'Ha' and then he says 'What!' Have you got it straight?"

"Maybe you better just glance over it again," said Bat.

Graves sighed and seemed undecided whether to repeat or bite off Bat's head.

"All right. You take this serum and these supplies on the riverboat *Nelson*. Then you—"

"The *Nelson*?" gaped Bat.

32

"Yes, the *Nelson*! Then you—"

"But that boat's skipper was the one that left me stranded at Mao-San! He's Slugger Owen!"

"Who else would *take* such a crazy trip!" snapped Graves.

"To where?"

"Oh, my saints and purple garters! To Fu-Chiang! To—"

"Hey!" yelped Bat, leaning up. "Fu-Chiang! Why, that's through all the battle lines and . . . and . . . why, the place is under siege, and even if you were cockeyed enough to get that far, you'd never get into the town!"

"Don't say you! *I'm* not taking the trip," said Graves. "You are!"

"But why Fu-Chiang?"

"Because," patiently, "Bill Fairington is there with the rest of the Americans at the consulate. The place has been under fire for weeks, and cholera has broken out and they need Cholera Serum Two. They have no money and are out of food. There are about thirty Americans and this Bill Fairington."

"Oh . . . then you . . ." Bat looked at Gwen Fairington—"you are here and helping finance this so I can bring him back—"

"We are going with you," said Gwen Fairington.

"I . . . I'm afraid so," fluttered Aunt Agatha.

"*You!* Through the battle lines? Through a siege—"

"It's front-page stuff," said Graves, smirking.

"Especially if they get killed," stated Bat. He seemed to be of a mind to argue the matter and then, seeing the cold, imperious way Gwen was regarding him, he didn't.

"Slugger Owen. Fu-Chiang. Cholera." Bat sighed. And

then he brightened. "Well, maybe it is front-page news, after all. If you'll excuse me I think I'll go get a dr— I think I'll have a talk with Slugger Owen."

"We sail this afternoon," said Gwen.

"Yeah," said Bat. "This afternoon."

"I'm afraid so," said Aunt Agatha.

The *Nelson*'s bottom was so thin you could almost see the bed of the river through it. The *Nelson* had once had a coat of paint. The stack had been riddled by snipers until more smoke came out the sides than through the top. She was a flat-bellied, five-ruddered, triple-screw, underpowered, overweighted, mis-built, lice-ridden, dirt-smeared, oil-fouled, wheezing, coal-burning, unmaneuverable old scow which should have been junked years ago.

Bat was all sadness, looking at her. She smelled of all the filth along the Yangtze, and she crawled with all the vermin ever to be discovered in China. And one night, with two shore batteries raging at her, she had lost steerageway upon a bar and just sat there and snored. And another night Slugger Owen had gotten drunk and abandoned Bat Conroy—

"Hello, Bat."

Bat found himself looking across a small space between dock and deck to Slugger Owen. The man was repulsive to him, and two or three times, in payment for that Mao-San deal, he had promised himself a chunk of Slugger's hide to nail upon a door. Slugger Owen was nothing much to look at, running mainly to fat and wearing long-sleeved underwear and pants and no shirt. He had carpet slippers upon his feet and a plain felt hat upon his head, which, it was said, had been given him by a Bund panhandler thirty years before. But for all that, there was power and brute force in Slugger Owen, for he stood at least six feet three, and the lard of him served as a protection to enormous muscles.

"So," said Bat, "we meet again!"

Slugger came to the rail and looked contrite, meanwhile blowing his nose in an unorthodox manner. "Now, Bat, you ain't never given me a chance to explain to you just what happened that night. You and me have been through too much together to be parted by one mistake. You and me have been pals. Honest to Pete, Bat, I'm just about the best friend you've got in these waters. Why, many's the time I've stood up for you in some dive. Yes, and slit a throat or two of them that'd malign your good name. You ain't gonna hold a thing like that agin' me, are you, Bat? Why, remember that pretty little missionary girl that I saved for you once—"

"That you *saved*!"

"I wasn't tryin' to kiss her, Bat. I was just tryin' to keep her from . . . from, well . . . I hate to say, Bat, but she was going through your grips—"

"A missionary girl going through my grips!"

"Sure!" said Slugger, his eyes aglow now with invention. "And I came in and—"

"How about that monte game? I suppose that holdout you had was planted on you by your Chinese cook!"

"Nope. By the mate, Bat, by the mate! Why, I'd go a long way afore I'd see you come to harm, Bat. Me and you—"

"Is pals! Now listen to me, Slugger Owen. You're a rotten,

whiskey-sotted, murdering thief and the last man in China that I'd trust with brass cash. But we've got two ladies coming aboard that dirty scow of yours and you're going to act like a gentleman or I'll cut out your heart, little by little, and feed it to a hog."

"Oh, now, Bat, that's bein' pretty hard on me that's the best friend—"

"Okay, *act* like my best friend! But one slip and I'll put so many little pellets in your guts that you'll have to be buried with a derrick! Be ready to sail by five this afternoon—if you can get that caved-in excuse for a garbage scow away from this dock!"

When Bat whirled and walked away, Slugger Owen grinned slowly to himself and then, in an excess of good feeling, booted a Chinese deckhand so hard that the boy almost went overboard.

"Sing!" roared Slugger. "You lousy brother of a pig! Get that cargo out from under that canvas and get it into the hold before that crazy Bat Conroy or them women get back here!"

And when the mate, Sing, went into action, yet another thing happened upon that dock which would have been shocking to both Slugger Owen and Bat Conroy.

A boy, ostensibly a coolie, carried the long cases with the others in the line. But before he had worked half an hour he slipped around the end of the godown and out of sight. A moment later he was writing a message to the Imperial High Command of the Japanese Expeditionary Forces in China. And upon his little face there was the utmost in satisfaction. He seemed already to hear bombing planes lashing down the sky and to see the water churned by shrieking shrapnel over what was left of the traitorous *Nelson*.

In detail, his message read:

RIVERBOAT NELSON, WHICH IS SAILING AT FIVE THIS AFTERNOON, IS VIOLATING THE SAFE CONDUCT WHICH WAS GRANTED BY OUR HEADQUARTERS TODAY. SHE IS CARRYING SEVERAL THOUSAND RIFLES, AT LEAST A HUNDRED MACHINE GUNS AND MUCH AMMUNITION. WOULD ADVISE SHE BE PERMITTED TO SAIL SO THAT SHE CAN BE DESTROYED WHEN NEAR DESTINATION, THUS ELIMINATING THE NECESSITY OF KEEPING FURTHER WATCH ON THESE ARMS AND ELIMINATING, ALSO, THE ACTIVITIES OF THE AMERICAN CAPTAIN OWEN. SIGNED J-42.

The *Nelson* wallowed along upon the restless jet bosom of the Yangtze Kiang beneath a smokily star-studded sky. Occasionally the creak of oars or the crackle of a sail and perhaps an illusive shadow marked other traffic upon the river. The old hulk pulsed loosely in tune with her thrusting pistons, and the sound of escaping steam and clanging shovels came from her fireroom. In the pilot house the worried face of the Chinese river pilot was a weird mask in the upthrusting glow from the binnacle. It was six hours upon its way, plowing against the current as upon a treadmill, through a lane in which flame and shell had left havoc where once quiet fields had stretched.

Bat Conroy stood in the radio room, where instruments with cracked and soiled faces told the Chinese operator secret matters. Bat was watching the yellow hands batter a message out upon a rickety typewriter.

CONROY
SS NELSON

THANK GOD YOU ARE COMING. WE HAVE BEEN WITHOUT FOOD, EXCEPT THAT WE CAN SCAVENGE. WE HAVE TWO CASES OF CHOLERA. THERE ARE NINE WOMEN AND FIVE CHILDREN HERE. THE SIEGE ON THE CITY IS TIGHTENING. HOW YOU WILL GET THROUGH THE BATTLE LINES I DO NOT KNOW. WE ARE PRAYING FOR YOU.

MORRISON
US CONSUL
FU-CHIANG

Bat ripped out the message, read it over again and then motioned his hand toward the key. "Tell them we will do our best."

Impassively the operator threw his switch and began to pound out the message. Bat, the paper in hand, went out on deck and glanced around. It was warm tonight, and as the wind was downriver he expected that he would be able to find Gwen Fairington on the foredeck. It was so dark that he almost fell over her chair before he saw her.

"Miss Fairington?"

"Oh . . . it's Mr. Conroy."

"I just got a message from Fu-Chiang, but it didn't say anything about your husband. Shall I try to contact them again and make sure he is all right?"

"Bill's all right," she said wearily. "He's probably dead drunk and oblivious."

"Beg pardon?" Bat said, not believing his ears.

She pushed a deck chair toward him and he sat down upon it. "You have been very sweet about all this, Mr. Conroy, and I feel that I had better tell you the whole story."

He felt very uncomfortable.

"Bill Fairington left me about three years ago," she continued in a low, unemotional voice. "I don't blame him. I was pretty much a child. Too much money, too little regard for his practice as a doctor. Whatever Bill Fairington is today, I have made him. I have searched for him for nearly a year, and each place I have gone the story is the same. Drink, women—he's been fired out of every job he was given, he has neglected his duty, he has embezzled funds—Well, I think I am the one responsible for it all. And so I have come to find him. When I do find him, I shall take him back to his own country. I've arranged, in a roundabout way, for a practice for him, and he'll never know that it was I that gave it to him. I robbed him of his self-respect. I didn't ever love him, I suppose. What I am doing now is a penance for having stolen a man's soul. That, Mr. Conroy, is the 'romantic' story behind this search. You can print it or not, as you like, but I only ask that you spare Bill's feelings as much as you can."

Bat Conroy sat staring at her through the darkness. He

hated to recognize the thoughts which were surging through his own mind. He tried very hard to be coldly professional.

"Then, when you do find Bill Fairington, it is to tell him that you are sorry for what you have done to him and are willing to do anything to make amends?"

"Anything but be his wife again. I have injured him too deeply."

A silence, cut only by the whisper of wind through the *Nelson's* neglected rigging, settled between them. And then, at last, she spoke.

"It must be very romantic, knocking around the Orient the way you do, on the trail of every battle, known from Russia to Cochin China."

"Oh . . . I wouldn't call it romantic. It's just hard work."

"Tell me about it."

He told her. He told her about nights in shell holes with corpses for bedfellows, about flaming towns and wretched civilians, about air raids and the way bombs sounded, about battles and the way bullets snicked and whispered and howled, and how to tell if an artillery shell was going to land on you or upon the next trench, about how it felt to be right in the middle of hot news and not be able to get out a word of it to the world. He told her about long and lonely roads, and sunsets, and Gobi raiders. He told her about Russians and Mongols. And then, realizing that he must have talked for hours, he suddenly stopped, self-conscious.

"I didn't mean to talk so much," he said.

But she was not so easily broken out of the spell which

he had woven about her and she did not answer. Her face was a small patch of white against the darkness, lighted a trifle, now that a few sparks soared from the *Nelson*'s stack. He saw that there was something like awe in her eyes, awe and perhaps—

Abruptly he stood up. "I've got to send another dispatch to Shanghai." And then, passing by her chair, the hand with which he guided himself touched hers. Did he imagine the slight pressure of that hand?

As he went down the deck, stepping over the snoring men off watch, his imagination broke through. How tired he was of kicking around China all by himself, with nothing ahead but more battles! To sit at a desk and receive the news and let the other guy do the work— He knew he could have a job in the New York office any time he asked for it. To think of wearing white shirts and riding in cabs!— A quiver of homesickness came over him. To eat salads with no fear of cholera. To drink real milk. To see white girls filling the streets and the blink-blink of movie signs, and to go to boxing matches. And—dared he think it?—to come home at night to somebody, somebody like Gwen Fairington.

He forgot about the dispatch. He wanted to be alone and dream out the rest of this tantalizing dream.

Slugger Owen was standing outside the texas and Bat nearly collided with him. "Oh, hello, Bat. Gee, Bat, ain't we the nuts? A boatload of fancy femininity and champagne—"

"Worry about things like that in Shanghai," said Bat, angry at having his reverie interrupted.

41

"Yeah. Yeah, sure. But you know, I ain't ever seen the like of that Agatha. Say, she's *something*! I'm telling her a pack of lies about things, and all of a sudden she up and says they're a pack of lies, and she almost threw me in the drink. She looks so darned quiet and scared, you'd never think she could take a man's ear half off with one twitch."

"Never mind Agatha. Get this tub upriver."

"Yeah. Yeah, sure, Bat. But of course you were just up forward there to smell the corpses floating downstream and you were there so long because a river devil—"

Bam! Slugger almost carried in the door of the texas when he went down. He couldn't exactly tell what had happened for a moment and then, as memory came back, he saw Bat standing in a determined way above him. He deduced that Bat had hit him and, feeling diplomatic at the moment, Slugger hitched himself so that he sat squarely on the step, as though he had gotten tired all of a sudden.

"—and if you don't," Bat was finishing, "I'll drown you!"

"Me and you," said Slugger, "have always been pals, Bat."

"Sure. We're pals as long as you get this tub upriver and try to stay sober. I'm not wearing this forty-five to keep my feet on deck."

"Okay, Bat. Sure, Bat. But it was all innocent. Honest it was. Ain't I always been a gentleman around ladies? And did I ever get drunk on duty? And have you ever heard anybody ever say a word agin my honesty?"

"Yes!" said Bat to all three questions. And he turned and strode angrily down toward his cabin.

Bam! *Slugger almost carried in the door of the
texas when he went down.*

He entered and switched on the light. He slammed and bolted the door. And then, still fuming, he stood in the middle of the small enclosure and massaged his right knuckles with his left hand.

The cabin was not much, containing a washstand and a cabinet, a locker and a chair, and two bunks—one so low that one fell into it and the other so high that anybody who might try to sleep in it had to be inserted there between mattress and upper bulkhead with great care, lest he be squashed.

Bat removed his coat and unbuckled his gunbelt. He rolled up his sleeves and turned to the washstand to get some grime off himself. But the washstand was dirtier than his hands, and he was just about to give it up when he noted something peculiar. In the mirror he beheld a bulge in the upper bunk.

Carelessly he moved to his gun. Swiftly he drew it and snapped, "Roll out or I'll *blow* you out!"

"Me?"

Bat gaped.

A blond head came out from under the blanket. Two startled blue eyes regarded the gun.

"You!" said Bat. "Again!"

She made a motion for him to point the gun the other way. "Are we far enough from Shanghai to have me put off?"

"Yes, damn it!"

"Good. Then it *is* I. Bat—"

"Get down!"

"Bat, I'm awfully hungry. I stowed away about four, and now it's midnight, and I haven't eaten since that breakfast you so kindly provided."

44

"What are you doing here?"

"I didn't know this was your room, Bat. I thought it was just an empty cabin."

His luggage, on the chair and under the bunk, was all marked, in large red letters—both in English and Chinese—"Bat Conroy."

"You're lying! Who are you?"

"Me?"

"You."

"My father," she said, "is a missionary. They're holding him upriver and I've got to go back and make sure he's safe."

"Yeah?"

"That's the honest-to-Pete truth, Bat."

"You're a spy."

"Oh, no, I'm not, Bat. Honest I'm not. I'm a missionary's daughter and I have to go back and make sure my broth—my father is alive. Don't you believe me?"

"Well . . . Why did you lie in the first place?"

"I told you that in the first place, but I guess you weren't listening. And then in Shanghai I didn't want to burden you—"

"What did you say your name was?"

"Huh?"

"Your name!"

"Oh, yes. It's . . . why, it's Lois Brant. That's it. Lois Brant."

"All right, Lois. I'll find you another cabin and let you stay. But by Patrick, if you change your name or your business again, I'll eat you for breakfast!"

"That would be nice."

"To be eaten?" Bat snapped.

45

"No, breakfast. Bat, I'm famished. Can't you get me something to eat? Just a little something? Even an anchovy!"

"Well . . . oh, hell, all right!" And slipping back into his jacket, he went out and dug up a steward.

Later, there were messages:

BAT CONROY
SS NELSON

TWO CHILDREN ARE ILL WITH CHOLERA
AND FOOD GONE. UNLESS YOU REACH US
TOMORROW IT WILL BE TOO LATE, FOR
WE CANNOT EVACUATE THIS CONSULATE
AND LEAVE THE SICK BEHIND US UNLESS
WE HAVE THE NELSON. HURRY!

MORRISON
US CONSUL
FU-CHIANG

BAT CONROY
SS NELSON

YOU STUPID BLUNDERER! YOU WORTHLESS
APE! WHAT HAVE YOU DONE NOW?
INTERNATIONAL SERVICE HAS RELEASED
THE STORY OF YOUR RIVER TRIP IN
FULL UNDER BYLINE PERRY LANE WITH
DAY-BY-DAY RECORD. HAVE JUST

RECEIVED THIS NEWS FROM FRISCO.
HAVE YOU SOLD US OUT? ARE YOU PERRY
LANE? YOU TRAITOR, YOU'RE FIRED!

> GRAVES
> SHANGHAI

GRAVES
WORLD PRESS
SHANGHAI

WHAT THE HELL DO YOU MEAN HAVE I SOLD
YOU OUT? HOW COULD INTERNATIONAL
SERVICE GET A DAY-BY-DAY RECORD OF
THIS TRIP UNLESS IT IS GUESSING ABOUT IT?
GO YAP AT INTERNATIONAL SERVICE AND
LEAVE ME ALONE, OR I'LL RUN THIS TUB ON
A SAND BAR AND QUIT!

> CONROY
> NELSON
> YANGTZE KIANG

CONROY
NELSON
YANGTZE KIANG

PUT A BOLD FACE ON IT, WILL YOU, YOU
RAT? FOR THE SAKE OF HUMANITY AND
THOSE KIDS IN FU-CHIANG, YOU KEEP
GOING OR I'LL CUT OUT YOUR HEART.
AND IF YOU FAIL TO GET TO FU-CHIANG

AND TAKE THOSE AMERICANS OFF I'LL
SEE THAT YOU ARE BLACKLISTED WITH
EVERY NEWS SERVICE IN THE WORLD
FOR A TREASONABLE, INCOMPETENT,
EMBEZZLING, FATHEADED, BLACKGUARD!

> GRAVES
> SHANGHAI

GRAVES
WORLD PRESS
SHANGHAI

YOU CAN'T TALK THAT WAY TO ME! I'LL
DELIVER THE NELSON AND THEN TO HELL
WITH YOU! I'M CARRYING ON FOR MISS
FAIRINGTON TO FU-CHIANG, AND THEN I
QUIT.

> CONROY
> NELSON

CONROY
NELSON
YANGTZE KIANG

YOU CARRY ON TO FU-CHIANG AND I'LL BE
NICE ENOUGH NOT TO BLACKLIST YOU.
SEND IN YOUR STORY AS YOU GO, BUT
AFTER FU-CHIANG YOU'RE THROUGH!

> GRAVES
> SHANGHAI

"I should worry," said Bat, reading the last message. "What the hell's been wrong with me for years I don't know! This is no job for a decent man, anyway. Following battles, ducking bullets, sleeping in mud, eating half-rotten food, taking orders from an old fool, risking my life today for headlines that will be ancient history tomorrow."

Gwen Fairington heard out his tirade, standing at the *Nelson's* rail beside him. "Poor boy, I wouldn't let him talk that way to me either!"

"I've shed blood in that service," said Bat, "and this is all I get for it! International fakes a story of this trip, and so I'm a traitor! Fu-Chiang and then—finish!"

Her deep, dark eyes regarded him thoughtfully. "You could probably get a good job in New York."

"Sure I could."

"And if you did—"

He prompted her, "And if I did?"

"Look at that junk!" she said, shifting the subject. "Good heavens, how do those poor coolies ever live through such labor?"

Bat regarded the coolies who strained along the bank of the gorge and didn't care a hoot about them. The big junk was twisting in the eddies of the swift-running stream. The coolies were straining at the line until the cords on their necks stood out.

This was a hell of a place, thought Bat. He'd been through these gorges two dozen times, yet each time they depressed him. The great yellow-red cliffs reared loftily, making man and his boats seem like frail toys. The strong force of the river thrust along its yellow flood, artfully covering sandbars and rocks. It was a cruel and merciless place, this China, and a man who spent his life here was fifteen kinds of a fool. Yes, he would leave. He would go back to New York. And Gwen Fairington—

"I'm not intruding, am I?" said the stowaway.

Well, that girl was here again—the girl with the face that was sweet, despite its boldness.

Both Bat and Miss Fairington looked at her in a detached way. She came and leaned on the rail on Bat's right. The wind whipped at the yellow hair which swept silkily out from under her beret and caught at her powder-blue cloak.

"Almost to Ning, aren't we?" she said.

"Pretty near," said Bat grudgingly.

"Above here, these gorges level down and spread out into plains, and then we come to Fu-Chiang. Right?"

"Yes," said Bat. And then, in sudden interest, "Say, Lois-Dorothy-Alice, you know this country pretty well, don't you?"

"I've lived in it since I was a little girl. My father once had a mission just ten miles south of Ning."

"Yeah. A mission!" said Bat.

"You know, Miss Fairington," she said, "sometimes I think Mr. Conroy doubts my veracity."

Gwen Fairington's eye, no matter how lovely and dark, might now have accepted the word "fishy" as descriptive.

"*Brrrrr!*" said the stowaway. "It's awfully cold in these gorges, isn't it?"

50

"Hmph!" said Gwen Fairington.

"Bat," said the stowaway, "didn't I hear you saying something about having received some radiograms to the effect that you'd lost your job or something?"

"You hear everything, don't you?"

"Not anything I don't want to hear," she said. "What was the matter about your job?"

"You wouldn't understand."

"I probably wouldn't, but I'm sorry. What did happen?"

"International Service—that's our rival agency in Shanghai—has been faking and running a day-by-day record of this voyage, and I'm accused of having sold out to them."

"Oh, gee, Bat, that's too bad. Are they awfully mad at you?"

"I haven't received any orchids, have I?"

"But can't you deny it or do something about it, or—"

"Sure. I quit as of Fu-Chiang."

"Oh, you mustn't do anything like that, Bat!"

"Thanks for your advice."

"Oh, I know I don't know anything about your business, but I'm sure you shouldn't quit."

"I'm fired anyway."

"I'm so sorry, Bat. Honest, I am! Gee, I wish I could help you!"

Gwen Fairington said, "Hmph!" again.

"Brrrrr," said the stowaway. "Well, I better be idling along. Don't forget to call me for dinner."

"She's quite impossible," said Gwen when Lois-Dorothy-Alice had left.

"Her? Oh, I wouldn't say that," said Bat.

"She's . . . well, too bold."

"Oh, she means all right. She's got a lot of nerve, but then, you need a lot of nerve in this country, and she seems to have lived in it all her life."

"That's probably what makes her so coarse."

"Coarse? Oh, come off! She isn't coarse. She's a good sport. You just don't understand her, that's all. She's very intelligent and she talks wise sometimes, but she's a good sort. Not bad-looking either."

"Hmph!" said Gwen Fairington. "I feel the cold myself now. Shall we part and meet at dinner?"

At dinner that night, when all was served and eaten and taken away, and when Slugger Owen, uncomfortable in a clean white coat, had gotten down to telling about what great pals he and Bat were, the radioman came in, impassively bearing a gram for Bat. Bat, who had seen enough grams for the moment, let it lie beside his glass unread.

"So me'n him says to this general," said Slugger, "'It's all right for you to shoot at us, but by God—'"

"Slugger!" said Aunt Agatha sharply.

"Yes'm," said Slugger. "'—but by golly. General, you broke every single bottle we had aboard!' And so this general, he sends right out and gets a case and we had quite a party. I always says that apologies is all right for diplomats, but the only kind you can believe is the kind that comes in a bottle."

"That was General Djeer-san?" said the stowaway, at the other end of the table.

"Yeah," said Slugger.

"And that was last year?"

"Yeah, so what of it?"

"General Djeer-san was up at Kalgan nearly all of last year, especially August, and it must have been August because you said the reason you'd run on a bar with the *Nelson* was because the river was the lowest it had ever been."

"What's a few details?" said Slugger, with a snap of his fingers.

"By the way, Slugger," said the stowaway, innocently looking the length of the board from over the top of her glass, "how is your lifesaving equipment? Do the boats launch and everything?"

"Absolutely!" said Slugger.

"But how can they float if they've got holes in them?" said Lois-Dorothy-Alice.

"Holes?" said Slugger.

"Big enough to throw a camel through," said the stowaway.

"Nuts!" said Slugger.

"Nuts or bolts, old boy," said Lois-Dorothy-Alice, "I recommend that you repair them first thing in the morning."

"Why?" This shot from Bat.

"Well . . . I was reading my horoscope this afternoon and it said that on tomorrow's noon I was going to get very wet in a shipwreck."

She seemed to be totally oblivious of the effect this had on Gwen Fairington and so was hard put not to giggle when Miss Fairington turned slightly green.

"You ought to know better than to scare people to death," said Bat.

"My horoscope," said Lois-Dorothy-Alice, "never lies." She got up, and smiled pleasantly at them, and went away from there.

Slugger began to protest that his boats were all good and Aunt Agatha wrung her hands and said she just knew they'd never get back alive. Bat twirled his glass thoughtfully and, growing weary of their chatter, thought he had better read this gram.

Unwillingly, and with a scowl that grew deeper and deeper, he read:

CONROY
NELSON

YOU DOUBLE-DAMNED TRAITOR!
INTERNATIONAL SERVICE HAS
ANNOUNCED THAT ITS STORIES ARE
NOT FAKED AT ALL BUT COME DIRECTLY
FROM THE NELSON. YOU ARE FIRED. YOU
ARE FIRED, YOU ARE FIRED. DO YOU GET
THE POINT? YOU ARE FIRED!

GRAVES
SHANGHAI

At Mo-Chli, some fifteen miles north of Tangfan, four planes were warming upon the edge of a camouflaged drome. Their engines muttered protest against the early hour, and the whirling props drank in the crawling mist. The red circles of Japan had been lampblacked out, leaving no identity other than the shape of the planes themselves, which were Kawasaki light bombers.

A stunted officer, looking much like an Australian honey bear in his heavy flying clothes, walked down the line, making his final inspection. Having finished, he turned and entered a small, dazzle-painted tent where his colonel took his morning tea.

"Captain Shimoto reporting, sir," announced the officer.

"Your planes?"

"In good condition, sir, loaded with light bombs and fueled."

"Very good, Captain. Here are your orders."

Shimoto read them, his little face filled with misgivings. "But, sir, there must be some mistake. The *Nelson* is under United States registry, and yet here it says that she must be attacked from the air and sunk without a trace. It is impossible to sink such a vessel without leaving ample evidence, and I am sure there will be much trouble—"

"You are thinking that you may be court-martialed after it is done. Perhaps we may even announce that you *have* been court-martialed, Captain. But the Emperor himself will decorate you, even so. The *Nelson* is loaded with rifles, machine guns, ammunition and bombs destined for the Chinese army, which is moving up to relieve the siege at Fu-Chiang. This is a violation of our regulations and cancels the safe conduct for which the United States asked. They are treacherous people, those Americans. They talk peace and act war. The *Nelson* must be sunk."

"I thought, sir, that she was going to the relief of the

Fu-Chiang consulate, where many Americans have taken refuge from the Chinese armies."

"That is the story which was announced in order to trick us into letting the *Nelson* through. The lives of many of our brave troops are forfeit if the *Nelson* reaches her destination. Be sure, when you bomb her, to leave no way for her to work her radio. That is all, Captain."

"Yes, sir." Shimoto saluted and went back to his four planes. In swift sentences he outlined the attack which was to be made and gave the reasons. His pilots helped him up into his ship and then scattered to their own bombers.

In a lopsided V, the four planes roared down the field and churned the mist as they rose. They circled once and then headed southwest toward the Yangtze.

Me?" said Slugger to Aunt Agatha. "I never did a dishonest thing in my life, and I never told a lie." He looked sideways at her from his place beside the helmsman and gave his cap an authoritative jerk, the better to hide anything in his eyes which might give him away.

Aunt Agatha was perched upon the transom, which flanked the battered charting table. She looked long and searchingly at Slugger.

"Don't you believe me?" he pleaded.

"No, I do not," said Aunt Agatha crisply. "You are probably the most dissembling blackguard I have ever met in my life!"

"Aw, now . . . that's going pretty far!"

"And is very true," said Aunt Agatha. "You are a liar among

liars, and I have no doubt that you would steal the pennies from a dead man's eyes, to use your own expression."

"Awwwww!"

"But of course," she added, "you have never had any good influences."

"No, sure, that's true," said Slugger. "I ain't ever had anything even close to a good influence in my life. I've been throwed with the gutter scum for so many years I've almost forgot I was a gent. But since I've met you, I know how sinful I've been sometimes and I repent. If I only thought it would do any good— Look. You ain't heard me swear since last night. And I'll give up swearing completely. I won't ever swear—" He stopped and listened, and then thrust his head from a texas window and looked toward the horizon. "What the hell is that damn noise?" he yelled.

They had left the gorges in the night and progressed down through a gently rolling country—green and brown. The river wandered aimlessly and slowly upon a broad way. Reeds and swamps flanked it on either bank, and small groves of trees obscured small clusters of houses. The horizon was smoky yellow, and it was almost impossible to make out the source of any motor hum.

On the forward deck, Bat Conroy looked skyward. His battle-tuned ears could identify the angry whine of pursuit ships and the rumbling roar of bombers, and he was not long in recognizing the sounds belonging to Kawasaki light bombers. He whirled, some sixth sense of news value functioning, and sprinted up the ladder toward the texas, heading for the radio room behind it. He almost collided with the stowaway.

"Bombers," he said.

"Kawasakis," she said.

"They're too low to be up to anything good."

"There they are!"

Bat stared upriver and saw them. The four came swiftly, developing from black lines into double lines as their separate wings became discernible.

Slugger snarled from the texas, "They won't attack us. I've got an American flag the size of that whole awning painted aft. They can't miss it."

"They missed the *Panay*'s," said Bat.

He threw open the door of the radio room and spoke swiftly to the operator. "Contact somebody—anybody—and stand by. I've got a hunch."

Languidly the operator threw a switch and began to twiddle his bug. The sound of his spinning generators drowned, for the moment, the roaring engines.

Bat stared up at the dark ships.

"No insignia!" said the stowaway. "But they're Kawasakis!"

"Got anybody?" said Bat to the operator.

"No. No catch."

The planes had roared over, the leader lowest, evidently inspecting the *Nelson* to make sure it was the proper ship. The V overcarried about a mile downriver before it banked. Then it wheeled in formation and, even lower, came back.

"It's come for us!" cried Bat. "I was right! Get down, everybody! Operator! Haven't you got anybody yet?"

"No. No catch," said the imperturbable Chinese.

Bat raked the decks with his eyes and suddenly with horror, saw that Gwen Fairington was standing on the forward hatch. She had risen from her deck chair and seemed to be hypnotized by the oncoming ships.

"Get somebody!" pleaded Bat. "Tell them we are being attacked by Japanese planes without insignia. Understand?"

"Yes. Understand plenty."

That done, Bat dived down the forward ladder. The planes were an aching snarl in his ears. Forward he saw a door opening into the fo'c's'le. If he could just make that—

He threw his arm around the startled Gwen Fairington and hauled her by main force toward the door. The thunder of engines was directly above him. And then he heard a shrill whistle cut through the din, a whistle which went up in tone as the bombs lashed down.

Flame and spray burst over the *Nelson*. Something swept off Bat's hat. He gained the door and slammed it behind them. The whole vessel was shuddering as though it had received a mortal blow.

"You stay here!" said Bat to Gwen Fairington, hardly noticing that she had sunk down upon a case and was sobbing. "The darn devils! And us with safe conduct signed by Shimizu himself!"

He opened the door. Flame was spouting out of the side of the *Nelson*. A wounded Chinese was holding the stump which had been his arm and was screaming. Other crew members were trying wildly to untangle the lines and davits of the starboard boat.

Where was Lois-Dorothy-Alice? Bat demanded of himself. But certainly she could take care of herself. She was that kind of girl. There was Slugger in the wheelhouse, heading the vessel in toward the port bank with all the speed the old tub could muster.

"Bat!" wailed Slugger. "Get the cover off that winch up there!"

He must have gone nuts, thought Bat.

"Do what I *say!*" roared Slugger.

Bat swerved over toward the ladder and yanked at the canvas cover. His eyes were startled by the sight of an antiaircraft machine gun. Yes—and he heard one fire a burst from the after deck beyond the texas!

He'd seen enough of them used. He squatted on the seat and rocked the thing up to forty-five degrees. What the hell was Slugger doing with antiaircraft machine guns? That made the *Nelson* a legal target, for an armed merchantman is considered a ship of war.

The four planes were coming back again, lower than before. Two Chinese crewmen appeared beside Bat and began to feed the belt into the gun. He pulled back the loading handle and then tried to adjust the sights.

The planes got bigger. From their snouts came stabs of flame as they raked the decks. Bat got the machine gun going. The tracer was arcing up to mark the path of his bullets and he made the path coincide with the onrushing leader. From the Kawasaki burst a black cloud of smoke speckled with flame. Bat tried to shift and get the second in line, but he could see no effect.

The after machine gun was also going, but the only plane hit was the leader. There came a loud explosion as bombs burst on their side. The *Nelson,* turned at right angles to the river, presented the narrowest possible target. But fragments screamed in the air and the starboard boat was a mass of splinters.

The three planes zoomed for altitude. The fourth went wobbling off, wheels brushing the reeds. It cartwheeled and exploded. The sound of its burning could be heard the instant the other three ships were at their farthest point.

For blood, the three came back. But they were higher now, and unwilling to sacrifice another ship. From their bellies dropped their remaining bombs. Slugger attempted to get out from under, but the *Nelson* was slow at her helm. An instant before the bombs struck, the *Nelson* thrust her bow into the bank, throwing one and all headlong and knocking Bat from the gun. When he got back to it, his targets were gone.

The sound of flames was louder now. Bat looked aft and saw that the radio antenna was gone and that the shack itself was beginning to burn. The operator, as he looked, went overboard in a feet-first dive, to flounder to shore on the heels of the swiftly departing crew.

"Damn it!" roared Slugger. "Somebody get some hoses! Do you want the whole ship to burn?"

Bat struggled with an old coil of canvas fire hose and finally got it hooked. The pumps were going below, thanks to the tenacity of the German engineer, and a hard stream of water played over the vividly blazing deckhouse. Slugger manned the hose with Bat, but only for a moment. Slugger suddenly dashed down a hatchway. A moment later, great clouds of steam and greasy smoke almost covered the *Nelson,* but the source was the stack. The cloud, in this windless portion of a riverbend, hung low on the water.

Bat gave the hose to two Chinese and then floundered through the choking fog until he found Gwen Fairington. He led her forward and dropped her at the end of a rope to the muddy bank.

He came back and found Slugger pawing through the mist.

"Where's Agatha and Lois?" said Bat.

"Just put them over the side. Boy, ain't this a sweet screen? I'll bet they think we're on fire through the whole ship! And all I did was throw in some tetrachloride bombs and shut the drafts. Herman is still down there—"

"What the hell are you doing with tetrachloride bombs?"

"Why, from the cargo, of course!"

"Cargo!" Suddenly Bat was very calm and deadly. "Slugger Owen, what's in this cargo?"

"Why . . . ulp . . ."

"Guns, I'll bet. Guns! No wonder they tried to blow us to smithereens! And now we're high and dry, and nothing short of a flood could get us off. We're licked! What about Fu-Chiang? What about those kids and those people?"

"Honest, I never—"

Bat flung him half across the deck. He would have followed up, but Slugger got himself lost in the smoke and Bat was left raging, without anything upon which to vent his wrath.

That serum was below in his cabin, packed in vacuum bottles and dry ice. He'd get that through. He'd have to do that much. He fumbled his way to his door and located the package.

From the shore came a hail in Chinese, and then what sounded like a truck engine. Bat dropped over the bow and floundered through the reeds until he came upon the group of survivors. But there were newcomers there, and on the muddy road stood a small convoy of armored trucks.

Slugger was talking animatedly with the officer.

"But I tell you it's all intact. I said I'd deliver it and I did."

"She is not on fire then?" said the officer, puzzled. "All this smoke—"

"I threw in a case of smoke-screen tubes," said Slugger. "She ain't burning."

"Ah," said the officer. "Then I shall have a number of trucks sent immediately from the main command. We are encamped about five miles from here, and I was on patrol when I saw the smoke of a boat. I thought it might be the *Nelson*—"

Bat sat down upon the earth and was so mad he came close to weeping. He hadn't gotten out the story, and he'd lost the *Nelson*. The last chance of his being sent to the New York office was gone, it seemed, unless he got this stuff to Fu-Chiang by night—and Fu-Chiang was still fifty miles away and surrounded by battle lines.

The stowaway sat down beside him. "Tough lines, Bat."

"Yeah."

"Does it lick you?"

"Lick me?" And suddenly he felt his madness turn into determination. "No, it does not lick me." He grabbed the officer by the tunic. "You're taking me to your general, my friend. Right now!"

General Chen-Li-Ki was very polite. He was as polite as any man can be when confronted with the kind of anger that Bat Conroy could turn on.

Cold and tough, Bat Conroy was saying, "They were your guns and you knew about the plan!"

"Oh, no. I had no idea such a method of delivery would be chosen. My superiors—"

"You and your superiors are in a tough spot," said Bat. "You interfered with a mission which is being spread all over the newspapers of the world. There isn't a man or a woman that can read that doesn't know the reason the *Nelson* was on her way to Fu-Chiang. And yet you jeopardized the lives of the Americans there by making it necessary for the Japanese to bomb that ship. For some reason, the people of the United States are in favor of the Chinese. When it gets out that you deliberately tried to murder—"

"Oh, no, no! Not at all! I did not know—"

"And the world," said Bat, "is going to know all about it. Tomorrow or the day after, the people of the United States are going to spit on your name."

"But there must be some way—"

"There might be."

"Ahh!" said the general, mopping his brow. "Then there *is* a way!"

"Give me the use of your radio and an armored car. Right now!"

"The radio certainly. The car— You cannot mean, Mr. Conroy, that you are going to go through the lines without getting special permission from the Japanese and then the Chinese in Fu-Chiang. It will take only three or four days to—"

"Meanwhile Americans are in there dying!" said Bat.

"But in such a war as this—"

"They've no business to have stayed there," said Bat. "I know that story. But they *are* there, and your damned armies wouldn't let supplies be sent through to them because those supplies might be used by the other side. I had permission to take the *Nelson* through, but I'm not going to hang around for a week waiting for permission to walk through. I want an armored car!"

"But we will have relieved Fu-Chiang in a week—"

"I want an armored car!"

"But it might fall into Japanese hands and be used against us. And if they fire upon it, you might be killed. And if—"

"If I don't get that car, tomorrow all America will spit on your name!"

"Oh, my! Captain, please take Mr. Conroy out and give him an armored car. But no driver, mind. Just an armored car."

"And the radio?"

"Yes, if you don't let America know—"

"I promise nothing, but I'll try to go easy on you. Good day, General."

"Good day," said the general. And when Bat had gone, "So that's the great Conroy! By Buddha, Lieutenant, he is a fool!"

Which, an hour later, seemed to be confirmed by Shanghai.

CONROY
TWENTY-THIRD ROUTE ARMY
EAST OF FU-CHIANG

SCOOPED, YOU IDIOT! WHAT THE
HELL IS THIS STORY TO ME NOW WHEN
INTERNATIONAL SERVICE GOT IT ON THE
CABLE SIX HOURS AGO WITH COMPLETE
DETAILS OF THE BOMBING? IT IS EVEN ON
THE STREETS HERE IN THE LOCAL RAGS,
DOWN TO THE LAST DETAIL. YOU HAVE
SOLD US OUT. I AM GOING TO BLACKLIST
YOU WITH EVERY NEWSPAPER IN THE
WORLD. YOU'LL NEVER GET ANOTHER
JOB SO LONG AS YOU LIVE. I AM CABLING
NEW YORK OFFICE FULL DETAILS OF
YOUR TREACHERY. I NEVER WANT TO SEE
YOU OR HEAR FROM YOU AGAIN. NOW I
KNOW THAT YOU ARE PERRY LANE, YOU
SWINDLER!

GRAVES
SHANGHAI

Smudged and stained and rumpled, Bat Conroy stalked through the Chinese camp with hell in his heart. How in the name of heaven could that story have gotten through? Perry Lane? How could Perry Lane have known about that?

Blacklisted with the world's papers, he was through! No dreaming now. Nothing.

He stopped by the tent where Gwen Fairington and her aunt were resting. Gwen got up from the cot, startled by his appearance.

"What's happened?" she cried.

"To hell with what's happened! I'm going through anyway, whether anybody ever published the story or not!" He gave her the message.

"But, Bat," said Gwen, "you shouldn't worry about this. I can buy you a dozen newspapers!"

"I know," said Bat. "But you couldn't buy back my self-respect unless I see this thing through."

"You mean you're going to . . . to try to crack the lines and get to Fu-Chiang?"

"Yes."

"But you may be killed!"

"That's the best part of it. You are staying here, and if Chen-Li-Ki relieves Fu-Chiang, you'll get into the town. Otherwise you may be able to get somebody to fly you back to Shanghai. Goodbye."

"Wait, Bat."

But he was already striding toward the idling armored car. He glanced around once or twice, not really knowing who he was looking for or why, but there was no sign of Lois-Dorothy-Alice.

The Chinese driver was standing with the door held open. There was a look of wonder upon his face and he seemed to doubt Bat's good sense.

Bat crawled in and slammed the door. The car was not new, by any guess. It had been captured from the Japanese early in the war, and had a missing bolt for every day it had been in the field. It was uncomfortable and gaseous and wretched, but, by some miracle, might last out the trip. Bat had painted, while he waited for an answer to his story, three American flags upon it, but he had no faith in them as assurance of safety. The vacuum bottles were on the seat beside him, wrapped in a coat.

He glanced over his shoulder into the back of the car, but all the plates were bolted shut and it was dark. Well, it didn't matter whether the thing mounted a machine gun or not. If the Japanese got him wrong, he'd never have a chance to use it.

He threw it into gear and, engine wheezing, it lurched ahead. He guided it out upon the road and opened the accelerator. The hard tires began to throw back fine sprays of mud.

About four o'clock he came in sight of the Japanese lines. Dull tents were spread out in a shiftless sort of camp which stretched in a careless semicircle about the recalcitrant Fu-Chiang.

The old walls of the town were still standing, for at this time of year it was very hard to operate artillery on the plains and the only battering had come from a small Japanese gunboat on the river and had done little damage to the thick mud walls.

Bat did not ask himself any questions. He speeded up as he came near the first outposts, and when two sentries, suddenly discovering that he was not a Japanese car (for he bore no rising suns), leaped into view from a ditch, he almost struck them. They dived hurriedly away and sent up a wail.

He was running between tents now, and soldiers, leaping away from the speeding juggernaut, were too anxious for their own lives to find their guns. But the hubbub had begun and it raced faster than the dashing car.

Because the Chinese had not sallied, there were no trenches, but only a few sandbag machine-gun emplacements facing Fu-Chiang. A scattering of one-pounders, any one of them throwing a shell big enough to stop the armored car, was also apparent to Bat's practiced eye, however fast the landscape was blurring. He was making about fifty over rough terrain and he estimated that he might get halfway across the open between the lines before they could start shooting at him.

He nearly left the ground whenever he struck shell breaks in the pavement, and the old car jarred and rattled its protests. To the right and left he saw the last two machine-gun outposts before Fu-Chiang. The alarm had soared this far and the blazing snout of one gun nearly scorched what paint the car had left. The sound of the striking bullets was deafening inside.

And then he was speeding out into the open, slamming along a gutted roadway which led toward the battered gates, going over and into and around shell holes like a jackrabbit filled with jumping beans.

A fountain of mud and smoke leaped up to the right and ahead. He ran through the flame of the next. Wildly he tried to zigzag and so throw them off. Shrapnel and bullets clanged on the armor like hammers on a dozen anvils. All it needed was one direct hit from a one-pounder and he was through—for keeps.

The gates were getting bigger and he was more than halfway.

The car seemed to crawl, though the distance was less than a hundred yards now, and in a few seconds—

The Chinese, excited, and fearing a trap, opened fire over the gate. The windshield became a white sheet, splintered by slugs. Flying glass gashed his face. A bullet came through and nicked his shoulder.

They weren't opening the gates. It was too late to slow down. He saw the mighty portals cover the whole world before him, and then, just as he cut the switch, everything turned red and white and black and his ears were deafened by the noise of the collision.

He fought to keep consciousness. He tried to see. But he could hear only the babble of voices and get the faintest glimpse of yellow faces all about him.

A familiar face, though bruised now and crowned by a shining tangle of yellow hair, was near his own and a familiar voice was crying, "Are you all right?" And then the face was volleying Chinese in a nearly hysterical voice and soldiers were trying to lift him from the shattered wreckage.

He concentrated on the face and wondered vaguely about the tears in the eyes. And then he tried to grin, despite the pain those busy Chinese hands brought him.

"You again!" he whispered.

And then the lights went out.

Bat could not get a grip on time, though he knew that much of it was passing, and he had an occasional, smoky vision of two faces, one or the other, or both. One was bearded and haggard but full of determination; the other was young and beautiful, and somewhat frightened. He was restless. He knew that he had to do something, but somehow he could not find exactly what it was. And so time slipped by him until, one day he found himself lying on a cot in a quiet room which seemed to have been an office.

The door opened and an overworked young man came in. "Ah," he said when he saw Bat blinking at him, "so you've come out of it! I eased up on the morphine this morning and I thought you would."

"Who are you?"

"I'm Dr. Fairington."

"You . . . you don't look like a drunken bum," said Bat thoughtfully.

Fairington grinned at him. "So you know the old rep, do you?"

"What happened to me?"

"You had a nasty concussion and I had to maul your skull a little, and then, knowing you'd probably want to be up and going, I set your arm and sewed up your chest and filled you full of morphine so you'd stay still."

"How long have I been here?"

"Five days."

"Five days! Holy mackerel! My story!"

Dr. Fairington looked puzzled. "What about your story?"

"I haven't filed it or anything! It was my one chance—!"

"There, there . . . now take it easy!"

"Where's everybody?"

"You mean my wife? Why, when the Chinese took the siege off yesterday, she came. Just about the same time the *Nelson* arrived. And thank God it *did* arrive—"

71

"The *Nelson*?"

"Certainly. I think dear old Agatha has some kind of strange power over a big brute they call Slugger. Seems that she practically browbeat him into getting the *Nelson* afloat and up to us."

"But the food . . . the serum . . . !"

"We got the serum all right, thanks to you, and in time. And as for food—well, the Japanese were suddenly very polite and sent some through the lines, and the Chinese seemed to be too scared of something or other to swipe it. We got food shortly after you arrived, though I don't know why."

"But my story!" yowled Bat.

"Now be quiet! You can get up tomorrow, most likely. We're all leaving here on the *Nelson* then. You're in good shape." He fumbled in his pockets. "Oh, yes. Here's a radio I've had for days for you."

Bat snatched at it and was then afraid to open it for fear of what it would say. Finally he got up nerve.

CONROY
US CONSULATE
FU-CHIANG

CONGRATULATIONS ON GREATEST STORY
OF WAR. YOU BEAT INTERNATIONAL
SERVICE BY SIX AND A HALF HOURS. I
GUESS YOU AREN'T PERRY LANE, BECAUSE
YOU SCOOPED HIM, AND HIS VERSION
WAS A LOT DIFFERENT THAN YOUR
OWN—PRETTY TERRIBLE, IN FACT.

YOUR PAY IS BEING RAISED. WHY DON'T
YOU COME BACK AND TAKE A VACATION?
LOVE

GRAVES
SHANGHAI

"Here!" said Fairington, alarmed.
But Bat Conroy, *the* great Bat Conroy, had fainted.

On the following day, late in the afternoon, a happy and
relieved party of Americans was boarding the singed *Nelson*.
Bat Conroy, his arm in a sling, stood on top of the crumbling
wall and watched them go. In his pocket was confirmation
of his request.

CONROY
FU-CHIANG

THINK YOU ARE NUTTY NOT TO COME
BACK, BUT IF YOU SAY THERE IS A GOOD
STORY BREWING NORTH OF THERE I WON'T
DETAIN YOU. DO ANYTHING YOU LIKE.
YOU'RE A HERO. YOUR SECOND AND THIRD
STORIES WERE EVEN BETTER THAN YOUR
FIRST, AND WE HAVE FULL CONFIRMATION
FROM JAPANESE AND CHINESE SOURCES
AND HAVE PRINTED THEM. DO ANYTHING
YOU LIKE. LOVE

GRAVES
SHANGHAI

73

It was a cheering message, of course, but today Bat Conroy was not capable of being cheered. Bat was very blue. For down there, arm in arm, went Gwen Fairington and Dr. Fairington, perfectly reconciled, perfectly happy. Their thanks still rang in his ears, but the tone of their voices as they spoke to each other wiped out forever any vision of a desk in a New York Office and the opera and salads and Gwen Fairington waiting for him to come home.

They were all going—Slugger with Aunt Agatha bossing him around, and a very changed Slugger he seemed to be. The crowd of battle-jarred Americans—

He wondered briefly what had happened to Lois-Dorothy-Alice or whoever she was. He had not seen her anywhere, and though he seemed to recall that she had ridden with him in that armored car unknown to him, he could not even be sure of that.

There went all his dreams!

The wind rumpled what hair escaped from beneath the bandages and pressed his trench coat against his legs behind and fanned it out before. He felt, standing there on that wall, very, very much abandoned and useless. Credit for three stories he had *not* written. Discredit for ten or more he *had* written. What a crazy business he was in! No business for any man with sense.

They were all aboard now and, even at this distance, he could hear Slugger bawling orders to cast off. Gwen and Dr. Fairington, on the foredeck, waved to the solitary figure on the wall. But Bat Conroy turned away.

He was weak and sore all over, and he was shaking from

the reaction of having been taken so sharply off a drug. He felt lower than he'd ever felt before and found less sense in going on living.

He walked out through the gates to the north and kept on walking. There was a muttering thunder in the air which he knew was artillery. The Chinese had the Japanese on the run, but the Japanese would probably retire into a fortified zone and then there would be lots of smoke for a while, until the Chinese got tired. It would be a good battle.

Slowly, as he dragged along, the sound of the firing grew louder and louder, and then he was passing a Chinese battery which filled the sky with smoke and howling shells. They were not very big guns, but for once the Chinese seemed to have the edge of artillery, for only an occasional Japanese shell hit the road.

He was passing into the outskirts of a ruined village cluttered with the remains of the fleeing Japanese force. Ahead, small arms were crackling wickedly and a machine gun was laughing. Bat sloughed off some of his lethargy. Say, this wasn't such a bad show after all! Darn sight better than they were getting on the Western front. He quickened his pace and then quickened it again. Say, those Japanese were in a kind of tough spot, if he knew anything about such terrain. He'd better find the Chinese GHQ and get a line on what was going on.

A small shell burst up the road and then another slammed into an already-shattered wall. Bat withdrew for a little to a ditch and was almost startled out of his wits when he found somebody sliding in with him.

"*You!*" he said.

"Me," she said.

"Look, can't I ever shake you?"

"Nope."

The shelling stopped. He looked at her for a little while. There was something about her face which compelled interest. And there was a strange grace to her which—

He climbed out and went on down the road between the ruined houses. She stepped along a little behind him.

"Bat—"

"Go on home, will you?"

"Bat, I've got an awful confession to make."

"Go find a priest."

"Listen, Bat. You've *got* to listen!"

He slowed down, half his mind still on the battle ahead. The small arms fire was getting louder.

"Bat, you know that story about the relief of Fu-Chiang?"

"That I didn't write, yet got credit for? Yeah."

"Well . . . I wrote it, Bat. And I wrote the other two for you."

"You?"

"Me."

"But why . . . how . . . ? How could you write . . ."

"Bat, you mustn't be mad at me. I've tried to make it up to you."

She had all his attention now.

"Go on," he said grimly.

"Bat, you know all those scoops International Service got on you? And all the beats from the *Nelson* . . . ? You know, when you ran forward to get that Fairington woman out of the rain and I was by the radio shack, and I got almost the whole story out before the antenna came down—"

"What are you trying to tell me?"

"That . . . that I'm Perry Lane, Bat. I never liked the name 'Penelope,' so I signed my stuff 'Perry.'"

"Perry Lane? Why, he's got the reputation of being one of the hottest newspapermen in China! He's everywhere and into everything and—why, that guy's been beating me for four months or more. You? Perry Lane?"

"When you found me, I'd been caught using a Japanese radio to get out my stuff and I'd lost my papers. They wouldn't have got me shot, but it was awfully nice being saved by you. I was raised in this country, you know, until I was fifteen, and then I went to the States and to college, and I worked for years on the Chicago *News Guardian*. Then I came back here for International—"

"You are Perry Lane!" said Bat, in a stunned voice.

"There's my Chinese Army card," she said apologetically. "Oh, Bat, please don't be angry with me! For years I read your stuff and worshiped the very paper it was printed on and then . . . I don't know . . . I seemed to get such a lot of fun out of getting an occasional beat on you . . ."

Bat wasn't listening. All he could think of was the bewildering and incredible truth.

"You are Perry Lane!"

"Yes, Bat."

He looked at her flushed, pretty face, at the flowing silk of her yellow hair, at the way she stood there, battle cape flowing out in the wind. Perry Lane!

A shell burst down the road. A wall caved in not twenty feet from them.

"Come on," said Bat at last, in a joyous voice. "Come on, newshawk! We've got to get in on this battle!"

A shell blasted earth up the road, another blew out a section of a roof. And overhead bullets sighed and snicked.

"Oh, the monkeys have no tails in Zamboanga,
Oh, the monkeys have no tails in Zamboanga,
Oh, the monkeys have no tails,
They were bitten off by whales,
Oh, the monkeys have no tails in Zamboangaaaaaaa!"

Story Preview

Story Preview

NOW that you've just ventured through one of the captivating tales in the Stories from the Golden Age collection by L. Ron Hubbard, turn the page and enjoy a preview of *The Red Dragon*. Join soldier of fortune Michael Stuart, who is now wanted more dead than alive after a failed scheme to kidnap the last emperor of China. On the run from the government he takes on a job to hunt down a mysterious black chest full of priceless treasure—but it may be far more trouble than its worth, as Michael's journey turns to deep danger and travels the thin line between life and death.

The Red Dragon

"M Y dear Miss Sheldon, you must believe me when I say that Manchuria is no place for a lady!" Blakely patted a stray black hair in place and frowned for emphasis. "Even the thought of your being in that country alarms me."

Miss Betty Sheldon also frowned, though her eyes were more thoughtful than worried. Seated in the overstuffed armchair, she could look out over the roofs of Legation Street to the place where the Forbidden City gleamed red and yellow in the setting sun.

"Then," said Betty, in a low, vibrant voice, "I shall have to forego the pleasure of being a lady."

"You mean . . . you mean you're actually going to discard all my earnest advice and go along? Certainly you can't mean that! I understand, Miss Sheldon, that your father's death has left you greatly upset. You must place some faith in the judgment of others. You'd never be able to make the journey. The Japanese swarm over that country. There are bandits, and excessive hardships. There are long marches which are completely without water.

"I advise you once more, Miss Sheldon, to let me handle this. I will take the chart and go after the Black Chest. You need only to remain here in Peking while I make the journey.

Barring accidents, I should return within three months. After that, I am certain that you will have ample funds for your return to the United States."

Betty Sheldon gave Blakely a cool stare. He was tall and gaunt, and his hair was a sheet of black oilcloth glued to his skull. His shirt bore a wing collar, clean and starched, but his fingernails were filled with ancient, dry dirt. His eyes were brittle things which stared behind you, and never straight at you.

"Now let me get this straight, Mr. Blakely. You are to take the chart and bring the Black Chest to me at Peking. Then—"

"Then you will reward me with ten per cent of the sale price of the contents of this mysterious Black Chest and we'll call everything square."

Betty Sheldon shook her head in perplexity. Her corn-colored hair shimmered under the impact of a ray of light and her eyes were as unfathomable, as blue as the deepest portion of the sea. She was very little more than five feet three, and when Blakely climbed out of his chair and paced the room, she felt like Gulliver in Brobdingnag—smaller, in fact.

Blakely shook a bony finger under her small, pert nose and his voice sounded like an off-key baritone horn. "Miss Sheldon, I was young once myself. In fact, I am still young." He paused to brush imaginary dust from his black suit coat. "I know to what depths of folly the younger generation can stoop. This idea of yours is utterly ridiculous. You think—" he shook his finger again, and Betty thought she heard the bones rattle— "you think that you can saunter through Manchuria to this what-ever-it-is, dig a hole, pull out the Black Chest, and then saunter back through Manchuria and arrive in Peking intact. You think you could make your way, unaided, through a seething country, while having in your possession probably no less than a million dollars."

"I didn't say that the Black Chest was worth a million dollars," protested Betty from the depths of the chair.

"Well, no doubt it is. Perhaps it is worth more than that. I know it's valuable, or that old fool Sheldon—"

"I beg your pardon?"

"Eh? Oh, pardon *me*. That is what the natives called him. Anyway, Miss Sheldon, your father would never have risked his neck twice and yours once to try to get it out unless it was worth plenty. I'm convinced of that. He blew your entire fortune looking for it, didn't he?"

"That's beside the point, Mr. Blakely."

"Yes, to be sure. But once again, let me state that there are Japanese soldiers in that country. They are utterly lawless. They shoot on sight and kill for the sport of it. And then there are bandits who seek to wipe out every white person who arrives in their vicinity. Some of these bandits stand on rocks, like this." Blakely raised his arms and pretended to sight along a rifle. "And when they even see a dust cloud, they fire into it before they know who it is."

"Where are the sound effects?" asked Betty Sheldon.

"Sound effects! I am sure, young lady, that we were speaking of—"

"Never mind." She stepped away from the chair. Even with high heels and cocky hat she failed to reach his shoulder. "Never mind going over it again, Mr. Blakely. They sent me here from the US Legation. They told me you were a collector, a man schooled in these things. That you were in a position to give me valuable advice."

"Of course I am!" cried Blakely, staring behind her and patting his hair. His mouth was slack, the lower lip protruding.

"But I find upon speaking to you that you are interested in only ten per cent of the Black Chest. You place your price at ten per cent. That was not clever of you—it is too little pay. Fifty per cent might have drawn me into a bargain. The ten only showed me that you had determined to cut me out completely. Please don't trouble me further, and please do not mention this business to anyone." She went to the door and placed her brown gloved hand on the knob.

"But where are you going?"

A small, wicked light came into being behind her eyes. "I think I shall ferret out the Red Dragon and see what he can offer me by way of a bargain."

Blakely tottered. He clapped a hand over his forehead and fumbled for his chair, still staring at her, jaw slack. "The . . . the Red Dragon?"

She smiled, triumphantly. "Yes. The Red Dragon."

"That devil? You'd . . . you'd actually trust your chart to the . . . the Red Dragon? But he's no better than a thief! A white thief in a yellow land. He's despicable!"

"Nevertheless, I am going." She jerked the door open.

"But . . . but you're not going to carry your chart about Peking with you?"

"It's safest with me, Mr. Blakely." Her heels clattered down the winding wooden steps as though a sergeant major sounded cadence for her. At the bottom she glanced back long enough to see Blakely's blanched face peering out his door.

To find out more about *The Red Dragon* and how you can obtain your copy, go to www.goldenagestories.com.

Glossary

STORIES FROM THE GOLDEN AGE *reflect the words and expressions used in the 1930s and 1940s, adding unique flavor and authenticity to the tales. While a character's speech may often reflect regional origins, it also can convey attitudes common in the day. So that readers can better grasp such cultural and historical terms, uncommon words or expressions of the era, the following glossary has been provided.*

Australian honey bear: a koala.

binnacle: a built-in housing for a ship's compass.

blackguard: a man who behaves in a dishonorable or contemptible way.

brass cash: any of various Asian coins of small denomination with a square hole in their center.

bug: a high-speed telegrapher's key that makes repeated dots or dashes automatically and saves motion of the operator's hand.

Bund: the word *bund* means an embankment and "the Bund" refers to a particular stretch of embanked riverfront along the Huangpu River in Shanghai that is lined with dozens of historical buildings. The Bund lies north of the old walled city of Shanghai. This was initially a British settlement; later the British and American settlements were combined into the International Settlement. A building boom at the end of the nineteenth century and beginning of the twentieth century led to the Bund becoming a major financial hub of East Asia.

camion: a low flat four-wheeled truck.

carabao: water buffalo.

Changkow: Kaingsu or Jaingsu Province; a province of China, located along the east coast of the country, on the Yellow Sea.

Chiang Kai-shek: (1887–1975); military leader of the Chinese Nationalist Party that attempted to purge Communism from China and unite the country under one central government. Civil war broke out in 1927 between the Nationalist government and the Red Army led by Mao Tse-tung. China was also involved in intermittent conflicts with Japan since 1931, with full-scale war breaking out in 1937. In 1949, the Nationalist government's power declined and Communist control ensued, forcing the Nationalists from mainland China into Taiwan.

Cochin China: a region covering southern Vietnam. Originally part of the Chinese empire, it was made a French colony in 1867 and combined with other French territories to form French Indochina in 1887 with Saigon as its capital. It was incorporated into Vietnam in 1949.

davits: any of various cranelike devices, used singly or in pairs, for supporting, raising and lowering boats, anchors and cargo over a hatchway or side of a ship.

dazzle-painted: something painted with dazzle camouflage;

a camouflage paint scheme of complex geometric shapes in contrasting colors. Its purpose was not concealment but to make it difficult to estimate the target by creating a confusion with rangefinders that operated by lining up two half-images of the target. Dazzle camouflage was intended to make it hard to do this job because the clashing patterns would not look right in the rangefinder sights even when aligned.

dog bites man: the phrase comes from a quote attributed to *New York Sun* editor John B. Bogart (1845–1921): "When a dog bites a man, that is not news, because it happens so often. But if a man bites a dog, that is news."

drome: short for airdrome; a military air base.

emplacements: prepared positions for weapons or military equipment.

fo'c's'le: forecastle; the upper deck of a sailing ship, forward of the foremast.

Forbidden City: a walled enclosure of central Peking, China, containing the palaces of twenty-four emperors in the Ming (1364–1644) and Qing (1644–1911) dynasties. It was formerly closed to the public, hence its name.

foredeck: the part of a ship's deck between the bridge and the forecastle.

Frisco: San Francisco.

G-men: government men; agents of the Federal Bureau of Investigation.

Gobi: Asia's largest desert, located in China and southern Mongolia.

godown: a warehouse; a commercial building for storage of goods.

Gulliver in Brobdingnag: refers to a satire, *Gulliver's Travels,* by Jonathan Swift, in 1726. Lemuel Gulliver, an Englishman, travels to exotic lands, including Lilliput (where the people are six inches tall), Brobdingnag (where the people are seventy feet tall), and the land of the Houyhnhnms (where horses are the intelligent beings, and humans, called Yahoos, are mute brutes of labor).

holdout: playing cards hidden in a gambling game for the purpose of cheating.

jane: a girl or a woman.

Kalgan: a city in northeast China near the Great Wall that served as both a commercial and a military center. Kalgan means "gate in a barrier" or "frontier" in Mongolian. It is the eastern entry into China from Inner Mongolia.

Kawasaki: aircraft named after its manufacturer. Founded in 1918, Kawasaki built engines and biplanes in the 1930s, including fighters and bombers.

key: a hand-operated device used to transmit Morse code messages.

Legation Street: also known as the Legation Quarter; it was encircled by a wall and was a city within Peking exclusively for foreigners. It housed eleven foreign embassies and was off-limits to Chinese residents.

limber: a two-wheeled, horse-drawn vehicle used to tow a field gun or an ammunition box.

Manchuria: a region of northeast China comprising the

modern-day provinces of Heilongjiang, Jilin and Liaoning. It was the homeland of the Manchu people, who conquered China in the seventeenth century, and was hotly contested by the Russians and the Japanese in the late nineteenth and early twentieth centuries. Chinese Communists gained control of the area in 1948.

Mariveles: a town and the mountains located in the southern part of the Bataan Peninsula on Luzon, the chief and largest island of the Philippines.

Mex: Mexican peso; in 1732 it was introduced as a trade coin with China and was so popular that China became one of its principal consumers. Mexico minted and exported pesos to China until 1949. It was issued as both coins and paper money.

Mikado: the emperor of Japan; a title no longer used.

Mindanao: the second largest and easternmost island in the Philippines.

monte: a card game in which two cards are chosen from four laid out face up, and a player bets that one of the two cards will be matched in suit by the dealer before the other one.

newshawk: a newspaper reporter, especially one who is energetic and aggressive.

one-pounder: a gun firing a one-pound shot or shell. It looks somewhat like a miniature cannon.

Panay: USS *Panay,* a gunboat responsible for patrolling the Yangtze River to protect American lives and property. In 1937 *Panay* evacuated the remaining Americans from the city of Nanking after Japanese forces moved in on the city. While upstream the *Panay* was bombed and sunk, killing three men and wounding forty-three others. Japan claimed that they did not see the US flags painted on the deck of the gunboat, apologized and paid for loss and damages.

Peking: now Beijing, China.

Route Army: a type of military organization exercising command over a large number of divisions. It was a common formation in China but was discarded after 1938.

Scheherazade: the female narrator of *The Arabian Nights*, who during one thousand and one adventurous nights saved her life by entertaining her husband, the king, with stories.

scow: an old or clumsy boat; hulk; tub.

screw: a ship's propeller.

Shanghai: city of eastern China at the mouth of the Yangtze River, and the largest city in the country. Shanghai was opened to foreign trade by treaty in 1842 and quickly prospered. France, Great Britain and the United States all held large concessions (rights to use land granted by a government) in the city until the early twentieth century.

SS: steamship.

steerageway: the minimum rate of motion sufficient to make a ship or boat respond to movements of the rudder.

stew-bum: an old hobo wasted by alcohol.

Sulu Islands: island chain in the southwest Philippines.

tetrachloride bombs: white smoke bombs; such bombs are made from chemical compounds and are for use in signaling or screening.

texas: a structure on a river steamboat containing the pilothouse and the officers' quarters, so called because steamboat cabins were named after states. At one time Texas was the largest state, and as the officers' quarters were the largest, they were called *texas*.

tracer: a bullet or shell whose course is made visible by a trail of flames or smoke, used to assist in aiming.

transom: transom seat; a kind of bench seat, usually with a locker or drawers underneath.

White Russian: a Russian who fought against the Bolsheviks (Russian Communist Party) in the Russian Revolution, and fought against the Red Army during the Russian Civil War from 1918 to 1921.

wing collar: a shirt collar, used especially in men's formal clothing, in which the front edges are folded down in such a way as to resemble a pair of wings.

Yangtze: Yangtze Kiang; the longest river in Asia and the third longest in the world, after the Nile in Africa and the Amazon in South America.

Zamboanga: province and port city in the Philippines, on the island of Mindanao.

L. Ron Hubbard
in the Golden Age
of Pulp Fiction

In writing an adventure story
a writer has to know that he is adventuring
for a lot of people who cannot.
The writer has to take them here and there
about the globe and show them
excitement and love and realism.
As long as that writer is living the part of an
adventurer when he is hammering
the keys, he is succeeding with his story.

Adventuring is a state of mind.
If you adventure through life, you have a
good chance to be a success on paper.

Adventure doesn't mean globe-trotting,
exactly, and it doesn't mean great deeds.
Adventuring is like art.
You have to live it to make it real.

— *L. RON HUBBARD*

L. Ron Hubbard
and American
Pulp Fiction

B ORN March 13, 1911, L. Ron Hubbard lived a life at least as expansive as the stories with which he enthralled a hundred million readers through a fifty-year career.

Originally hailing from Tilden, Nebraska, he spent his formative years in a classically rugged Montana, replete with the cowpunchers, lawmen and desperadoes who would later people his Wild West adventures. And lest anyone imagine those adventures were drawn from vicarious experience, he was not only breaking broncs at a tender age, he was also among the few whites ever admitted into Blackfoot society as a bona fide blood brother. While if only to round out an otherwise rough and tumble youth, his mother was that rarity of her time—a thoroughly educated woman—who introduced her son to the classics of Occidental literature even before his seventh birthday.

But as any dedicated L. Ron Hubbard reader will attest, his world extended far beyond Montana. In point of fact, and as the son of a United States naval officer, by the age of eighteen he had traveled over a quarter of a million miles. Included therein were three Pacific crossings to a then still mysterious Asia, where he ran with the likes of Her British Majesty's agent-in-place

L. Ron Hubbard, left, at Congressional Airport, Washington, DC, 1931, with members of George Washington University flying club.

for North China, and the last in the line of Royal Magicians from the court of Kublai Khan. For the record, L. Ron Hubbard was also among the first Westerners to gain admittance to forbidden Tibetan monasteries below Manchuria, and his photographs of China's Great Wall long graced American geography texts.

Upon his return to the United States and a hasty completion of his interrupted high school education, the young Ron Hubbard entered George Washington University. There, as fans of his aerial adventures may have heard, he earned his wings as a pioneering barnstormer at the dawn of American aviation. He also earned a place in free-flight record books for the longest sustained flight above Chicago. Moreover, as a roving reporter for *Sportsman Pilot* (featuring his first professionally penned articles), he further helped inspire a generation of pilots who would take America to world airpower.

Immediately beyond his sophomore year, Ron embarked on the first of his famed ethnological expeditions, initially to then untrammeled Caribbean shores (descriptions of which would later fill a whole series of West Indies mystery-thrillers). That the Puerto Rican interior would also figure into the future of Ron Hubbard stories was likewise no accident. For in addition to cultural studies of the island, a 1932–33

LRH expedition is rightly remembered as conducting the first complete mineralogical survey of a Puerto Rico under United States jurisdiction.

There was many another adventure along this vein: As a lifetime member of the famed Explorers Club, L. Ron Hubbard charted North Pacific waters with the first shipboard radio direction finder, and so pioneered a long-range navigation system universally employed until the late twentieth century. While not to put too fine an edge on it, he also held a rare Master Mariner's license to pilot any vessel, of any tonnage in any ocean.

Yet lest we stray too far afield, there is an LRH note at this juncture in his saga, and it reads in part:

"I started out writing for the pulps, writing the best I knew, writing for every mag on the stands, slanting as well as I could."

To which one might add: His earliest submissions date from the summer of 1934, and included tales drawn from true-to-life Asian adventures, with characters roughly modeled on British/American intelligence operatives he had known in Shanghai. His early Westerns were similarly peppered with details drawn from personal

Capt. L. Ron Hubbard in Ketchikan, Alaska, 1940, on his Alaskan Radio Experimental Expedition, the first of three voyages conducted under the Explorers Club flag.

experience. Although therein lay a first hard lesson from the often cruel world of the pulps. His first Westerns were soundly rejected as lacking the authenticity of a Max Brand yarn (a particularly frustrating comment given L. Ron Hubbard's Westerns came straight from his Montana homeland, while Max Brand was a mediocre New York poet named Frederick Schiller Faust, who turned out implausible six-shooter tales from the terrace of an Italian villa).

Nevertheless, and needless to say, L. Ron Hubbard persevered and soon earned a reputation as among the most publishable names in pulp fiction, with a ninety percent placement rate of first-draft manuscripts. He was also among the most prolific, averaging between seventy and a hundred thousand words a month. Hence the rumors that L. Ron Hubbard had redesigned a typewriter for faster keyboard action and pounded out manuscripts on a continuous roll of butcher paper to save the precious seconds it took to insert a single sheet of paper into manual typewriters of the day.

That all L. Ron Hubbard stories did not run beneath said byline is yet another aspect of pulp fiction lore. That is, as publishers periodically rejected manuscripts from top-drawer authors if only to avoid paying top dollar, L. Ron Hubbard and company just as frequently replied with submissions under various pseudonyms. In Ron's case, the

A MAN OF MANY NAMES

Between 1934 and 1950, L. Ron Hubbard authored more than fifteen million words of fiction in more than two hundred classic publications. To supply his fans and editors with stories across an array of genres and pulp titles, he adopted fifteen pseudonyms in addition to his already renowned L. Ron Hubbard byline.

Winchester Remington Colt
Lt. Jonathan Daly
Capt. Charles Gordon
Capt. L. Ron Hubbard
Bernard Hubbel
Michael Keith
Rene Lafayette
Legionnaire 148
Legionnaire 14830
Ken Martin
Scott Morgan
Lt. Scott Morgan
Kurt von Rachen
Barry Randolph
Capt. Humbert Reynolds

list included: Rene Lafayette, Captain Charles Gordon, Lt. Scott Morgan and the notorious Kurt von Rachen—supposedly on the lam for a murder rap, while hammering out two-fisted prose in Argentina. The point: While L. Ron Hubbard as Ken Martin spun stories of Southeast Asian intrigue, LRH as Barry Randolph authored tales of

romance on the Western range—which, stretching between a dozen genres is how he came to stand among the two hundred elite authors providing close to a million tales through the glory days of American Pulp Fiction.

L. Ron Hubbard, circa 1930, at the outset of a literary career that would finally span half a century.

In evidence of exactly that, by 1936 L. Ron Hubbard was literally leading pulp fiction's elite as president of New York's American Fiction Guild. Members included a veritable pulp hall of fame: Lester "Doc Savage" Dent, Walter "The Shadow" Gibson, and the legendary Dashiell Hammett—to cite but a few.

Also in evidence of just where L. Ron Hubbard stood within his first two years on the American pulp circuit: By the spring of 1937, he was ensconced in Hollywood, adopting a Caribbean thriller for Columbia Pictures, remembered today as *The Secret of Treasure Island*. Comprising fifteen thirty-minute episodes, the L. Ron Hubbard screenplay led to the most profitable matinée serial in Hollywood history. In accord with Hollywood culture, he was thereafter continually called upon

The 1937 Secret of Treasure Island, *a fifteen-episode serial adapted for the screen by L. Ron Hubbard from his novel,* Murder at Pirate Castle.

to rewrite/doctor scripts—most famously for long-time friend and fellow adventurer Clark Gable.

In the interim—and herein lies another distinctive chapter of the L. Ron Hubbard story—he continually worked to open Pulp Kingdom gates to up-and-coming authors. Or, for that matter, anyone who wished to write. It was a fairly unconventional stance, as markets were already thin and competition razor sharp. But the fact remains, it was an L. Ron Hubbard hallmark that he vehemently lobbied on behalf of young authors—regularly supplying instructional articles to trade journals, guest-lecturing to short story classes at George Washington University and Harvard, and even founding his own creative writing competition. It was established in 1940, dubbed the Golden Pen, and guaranteed winners both New York representation and publication in *Argosy*.

But it was John W. Campbell Jr.'s *Astounding Science Fiction* that finally proved the most memorable LRH vehicle. While every fan of L. Ron Hubbard's galactic epics undoubtedly knows the story, it nonetheless bears repeating: By late 1938, the pulp publishing magnate of Street & Smith was determined to revamp *Astounding Science Fiction* for broader readership. In particular, senior editorial director F. Orlin Tremaine called for stories with a stronger *human element*. When acting editor John W. Campbell balked, preferring his spaceship-driven

104

tales, Tremaine enlisted Hubbard. Hubbard, in turn, replied with the genre's first truly *character-driven* works, wherein heroes are pitted not against bug-eyed monsters but the mystery and majesty of deep space itself—and thus was launched the Golden Age of Science Fiction.

The names alone are enough to quicken the pulse of any science fiction aficionado, including LRH friend and protégé, Robert Heinlein, Isaac Asimov, A. E. van Vogt and Ray Bradbury. Moreover, when coupled with LRH stories of fantasy, we further come to what's rightly been described as the foundation of every modern tale of horror: L. Ron Hubbard's immortal *Fear*. It was rightly proclaimed by Stephen King as one of the very few works to genuinely warrant that overworked term "classic"—as in: *"This is a classic tale of creeping, surreal menace and horror. . . . This is one of the really, really good ones."*

To accommodate the greater body of L. Ron Hubbard fantasies, Street & Smith inaugurated *Unknown*—a classic pulp if there ever was one, and wherein readers were soon thrilling to the likes of *Typewriter in the Sky* and *Slaves of Sleep* of which Frederik Pohl would declare: *"There are bits and pieces from Ron's work that became part of the language in ways that very few other writers managed."*

And, indeed, at J. W. Campbell Jr.'s insistence, Ron was regularly drawing on themes from the Arabian Nights and

L. Ron Hubbard, 1948, among fellow science fiction luminaries at the World Science Fiction Convention in Toronto.

so introducing readers to a world of genies, jinn, Aladdin and Sinbad—all of which, of course, continue to float through cultural mythology to this day.

At least as influential in terms of post-apocalypse stories was L. Ron Hubbard's 1940 *Final Blackout*. Generally acclaimed as the finest anti-war novel of the decade and among the ten best works of the genre ever authored—here, too, was a tale that would live on in ways few other writers imagined.

Portland, Oregon, 1943; L. Ron Hubbard, captain of the US Navy subchaser PC 815.

Hence, the later Robert Heinlein verdict: "Final Blackout *is as perfect a piece of science fiction as has ever been written.*"

Like many another who both lived and wrote American pulp adventure, the war proved a tragic end to Ron's sojourn in the pulps. He served with distinction in four theaters and was highly decorated for commanding corvettes in the North Pacific. He was also grievously wounded in combat, lost many a close friend and colleague and thus resolved to say farewell to pulp fiction and devote himself to what it had supported these many years—namely, his serious research.

But in no way was the LRH literary saga at an end, for as he wrote some thirty years later, in 1980:

"Recently there came a period when I had little to do. This was novel in a life so crammed with busy years, and I decided to amuse myself by writing a novel that was pure science fiction."

That work was *Battlefield Earth: A Saga of the Year 3000*. It was an immediate *New York Times* bestseller and, in fact, the first international science fiction blockbuster in decades. It was not, however, L. Ron Hubbard's magnum opus, as that distinction is generally reserved for his next and final work: The 1.2 million word *Mission Earth*.

> **Final Blackout**
> *is as perfect a piece of science fiction as has ever been written.*
>
> —Robert Heinlein

How he managed those 1.2 million words in just over twelve months is yet another piece of the L. Ron Hubbard legend. But the fact remains, he did indeed author a ten-volume *dekalogy* that lives in publishing history for the fact that each and every volume of the series was also a *New York Times* bestseller.

Moreover, as subsequent generations discovered L. Ron Hubbard through republished works and novelizations of his screenplays, the mere fact of his name on a cover signaled an international bestseller. . . . Until, to date, sales of his works exceed hundreds of millions, and he otherwise remains among the most enduring and widely read authors in literary history. Although as a final word on the tales of L. Ron Hubbard, perhaps it's enough to simply reiterate what editors told readers in the glory days of American Pulp Fiction:

He writes the way he does, brothers, because he's been there, seen it and done it!

THE STORIES FROM THE GOLDEN AGE

Your ticket to adventure starts here with the Stories from
the Golden Age collection by master storyteller L. Ron Hubbard.
These gripping tales are set in a kaleidoscope of exotic locales and brim
with fascinating characters, including some of the
most vile villains, dangerous dames and brazen heroes
you'll ever get to meet.

The entire collection of over one hundred and fifty stories is being
released in a series of eighty books and audiobooks.
For an up-to-date listing of available titles,
go to www.goldenagestories.com.

AIR ADVENTURE

109

FAR-FLUNG ADVENTURE

SEA ADVENTURE

TALES FROM THE ORIENT

The Devil—With Wings *Pearl Pirate*
The Falcon Killer *The Red Dragon*
Five Mex for a Million *Spy Killer*
Golden Hell *Tah*
The Green God *The Trail of the Red Diamonds*
Hurricane's Roar *Wind-Gone-Mad*
Inky Odds *Yellow Loot*
Orders Is Orders

MYSTERY

The Blow Torch Murder *The Grease Spot*
Brass Keys to Murder *Killer Ape*
Calling Squad Cars! *Killer's Law*
The Carnival of Death *The Mad Dog Murder*
The Chee-Chalker *Mouthpiece*
Dead Men Kill *Murder Afloat*
The Death Flyer *The Slickers*
Flame City *They Killed Him Dead*

FANTASY

SCIENCE FICTION

WESTERN

The Baron of Coyote River	*Man for Breakfast*
Blood on His Spurs	*The No-Gun Gunhawk*
Boss of the Lazy B	*The No-Gun Man*
Branded Outlaw	*The Ranch That No One Would Buy*
Cattle King for a Day	*Reign of the Gila Monster*
Come and Get It	*Ride 'Em, Cowboy*
Death Waits at Sundown	*Ruin at Rio Piedras*
Devil's Manhunt	*Shadows from Boot Hill*
The Ghost Town Gun-Ghost	*Silent Pards*
Gun Boss of Tumbleweed	*Six-Gun Caballero*
Gunman!	*Stacked Bullets*
Gunman's Tally	*Stranger in Town*
The Gunner from Gehenna	*Tinhorn's Daughter*
Hoss Tamer	*The Toughest Ranger*
Johnny, the Town Tamer	*Under the Diehard Brand*
King of the Gunmen	*Vengeance Is Mine!*
The Magic Quirt	*When Gilhooly Was in Flower*

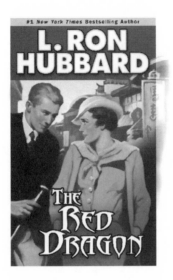

JOIN THE PULP REVIVAL
America in the 1930s and 40s

Pulp fiction was in its heyday and 30 million readers were regularly riveted by the larger-than-life tales of master storyteller L. Ron Hubbard. For this was pulp fiction's golden age, when the writing was raw and every page packed a walloping punch.

That magic can now be yours. An evocative world of nefarious villains, exotic intrigues, courageous heroes and heroines—a world that today's cinema has barely tapped for tales of adventure and swashbucklers.

Enroll today in the Stories from the Golden Age Club and begin receiving your monthly feature edition selected from more than 150 stories in the collection.

You may choose to enjoy them as either a paperback or audiobook for the special membership price of $9.95 each month along with FREE shipping and handling.

CALL TOLL-FREE: 1-877-8GALAXY
(1-877-842-5299) OR GO ONLINE TO
www.goldenagestories.com
AND BECOME PART OF THE PULP REVIVAL!

Prices are set in US dollars only. For non-US residents, please call
1-323-466-7815 for pricing information. Free shipping available for US residents only.

Galaxy Press, 7051 Hollywood Blvd., Suite 200, Hollywood, CA 90028